A Silver Tongue

a novel by

Marlene Taylor

Listen with your heart.
Marlene Taylor
Aug 2004

Oshun Dynasty Publications
Visit: www.asilvertongue.com

ALSO BY MARLENE TAYLOR

Life Is What You Make It, Darlin'

Published by Oshun Dynasty Publications
P O Box 2574 Bala Cynwyd PA 19004

First Printed, January, 2002
10   9 8 7 6 5 4 3 2 1

Publisher's Cataloging-in-Publication
(Provided by Quality Books, Inc.)

Taylor, Marlene.
       A silver tongue / by Marlene Taylor. -- 1st ed.
       p. cm.
       ISBN: 0-9677679-1-1

       1.   Women--Fiction.   I. Title.

   PS3570.A9454S55 2000   813.6

                  QB199-500587

DISCLAIMER:
This is a work of fiction. Names, characters, places and incidents
are either the product of the author's imagination or are used
fictitiously, and any resemblance to actual persons, living or dead,
events, or locales is entirely coincidental.

Acknowledgments

The psychological tone of this book was set with the help of one of my dearest friends, Dr. Claudia Kirkland Lyles. Thanks, buddy. My teenage children, Geneva and Veronica, worked by my side, cheering me on and assisting me in various ways, throughout the entire course of this project. I couldn't ask for better kids.

My thanks go out to Ellie Conrad, fellow author and helpful editor for her initial insightful comments. And, Diane Lockett, teacher, poet, and author. Also my final editor and proofreader—it wouldn't have been the same without you. Thanks to you both. Damali Kenya, my very talented young graphic designer, you're amazing!

These acknowledgements would not be complete without an expression of gratitude and awe for my mother, Dorothy Harris. None of this would have been possible without you, Joe S., Attorney Dan Childs, and Dr. William King, all generous patrons of the arts; thank you all for your unwavering support.

I would also like to thank the many faceless domestic abuse researchers for making available reports containing analytical information, which also helped to frame the context of this book.

Thank you; all of you pioneering women out there, for the work you have done in bringing this issue of domestic violence to the forefront so that we may find a way toward a positive solution.

Most of all, thank you, dear reader, as a portion of the proceeds from the sale of this book is being donated to women's shelters around the country.

-- *Marlene Taylor*

Dedications

This book is dedicated to my network of family, friends, associates and fellow authors who have supported my efforts, either directly or indirectly. I hope not to leave out anyone, but if I do, please know that you are loved, nonetheless. I wish to dedicate this work to my sisters, Terry, Kathy, & Kim, Pat Alexander, Phil Allen, Cody Anderson, Dr. Monica Anderson, Karen Austin-Williams, Nicole Bailey-Williams, Dr. Linda Baker, Edwina Baker, Arline & Jenna Balaban, Roland Banks, Damon & Debbie Barr, Chuck Barsh, John Batts, Marion Beaufort, Brian Bell, Kathy Bellamy, Ernest Bernard, Kim Berry, Bil & Val Beverly, Bruce & Theresa Beverly, Steven & Felisha Beverly, Ernie & Tangie Bley, George & Martha Blood, Bill Blue, Carter Borden, Walter Borum, Lynn, Skeets & Dennie Bowser, Mary Boxley-White, Dave & Yvonne Branch, Odun & Jamil Brannen, Curnel Bridges, Sandra Broadus, Beatrice Brown, Carla Brown, Jeff Brown, Nancy Caldwell, Bernice Calvin, Tomlin Campbell, Lorene Carey, Thornton Caroll, JC Carter, Althea Caruth, Linda Chandler, Lillian Chase, Cassie, Jasmine & Tyler Chatman, Augusta Clark, Tony Clay, Roz Cofer, Susan Cohen, Rick Coley, Annette Collier, Danielle Cook, Walter & Mildred Council, Terry & Wanda Crockett, Lisa Cross, Vicki, Stanley, Birdie, Jackie, Sieda, Neema, Oscar, Squeaky, & Rashid Culbreth, Bridget Cunningham, Aliyah DaCosta, Julia Davis, Rosalie & Wesley Day, Danielle Dempsey, Toni Dennis, Henry & Alma Dillard, Aneita Duglas, Verna Edwards, Alethia & Val Erwin, Nancy Ewell, Larry Farmbry, Anthony Farrow, Monique Ford, Ronald & Darrin Foster, George Fraser, Nate Gadsden, Ebony & Shaquille Gaines-Tyler, Chuck Gamble, Harriet Garrett, Rhonda Gibson, Dennis Glenn, Vicki & Felicia Gooden, Liz Gore, Linda Gray, John Greenlee, Pam & Jimmy Griffin, Greg Hammond, Phyllis Harden, Rufus Harley, Stephanie Harrell, Brenda Harris, Charles Harris, Jeffrey Hart, Earl Harvey, Mustafa Hashim, Malika & Yusef Havard, Dean Hayman-Mason, Alan & Ellen Heavens, Doug Henderson, Tamlin Henry, Mary Hewlett, Mr. & Mrs. Alfred Hill, Kelly & Leon Hinman, Al Hunter, Wayne Hunter, Dave & Dee Dee Hyman, the late Ethel Ivery, Edwardo Jackson, Marie Jackson, Garland Jaggers, Revere James, Veronica Johnson, Audrey Johnson-Thornton, Angelique Jones, Curtis Jones, Hanford Jones, Mary Jones, Rhonda & Paulette Jones, Terry Tariq Jones, Keith Jordan, Mike Joynes, Barbara

Keaton, Cecilia Keller, Myeung, Carol & Han Kim, Clifford King, Rosalee Lacey, Vicki Leach, Dr. Susan Leath, Rotan & Gracie Lee, Michele Leftwich, Gwen Lewis, Sandra Long, Tawanda Longs, Dr. Carol Love, Thera Martin, Cheryl McCallister, Clarice McGilberry, Mark McGill, Adrienne McKinney, Traci McKinley, Geri McReynolds, Larry Miles, Karen Miller, Morgan Miller, Michelle Mitchell, the late Dr. Howard Mitchell, Mertine Moore, Roscoe Murphy, Rep John Myers, Imari Obadele, Donna & John Ollison, Maria Pajil, Kathy Parker, Sheila Parker, Phil Parrish, Eileen Perez, Johnathan, Che, Lynda, Daren & Ken Perry, Dicky Peterson, Zandra Price, Tracy Price-Thompson, Blondell Reynolds, Gwen Richardson, Robbertto Rickards, Betty, Dianee and Sharon Roberts, Chuckie, Renee, Lois-Jean, Bobby & Billy Roberts, Doris Roberts, Gregory & Evelyn Roberts, Kenny & Thomasina Roberts, William & Carol Roberts, Larry Robin, Carole Robinson, Nochie Robinson, Ruby Robinson-Kilpatrick, Emma Rodgers, Evette Rodgers, Rev Gus Roman, Dr. Denise Ross, Bruce Rush, Kosmond Russell, Sameerah Shabazz, Steve Sattel, Joan Schley, Joyce Schofield, Pandora Seaton, Marilyn Sessoms-Horsey, Daryl Shore, Althea Singleton, Brenda Singleton, Karl Slater, Dave & Teddy Smith, Diane, Donna, Berta & Bobbsie Smith, Leah Smith, Norma & Butter Smith, Paula Smith, Sherry Smith, Dexter, Elmina, Leesil, Dawn, Sasha & Vicky St. Hillaire, Etienne & Makaela Starling, Vera, Miko, Butchie, & Kissy Starling, Francine Swanier, Bernadette & Lonni Tanksley, James & RaJean Taylor, Jonathan, JoAnn & Gerard Taylor, Eric Teel, Carmela Thomas, Dr. Lynda Thomas, Marzella Thomas, Renee Thompson, Vinnie Thompson, Janice Truehart-Beasley, Sharon Tucker, Barbara Turner, Jackie Tyler, Barbara Wallace, Jeanette Walton, Gabrielle Wanamaker, Zenobia Waridi, Lecia Warner, Rep LeAnna Washington, Joyce & John Waters, AM Weaver, Jeff West, Ellen White, Jeff White, LaVerne Wiggins, Marc Williams, Sonia Williams-Babers, Victoria Wilson, Sue, Bill & Molly Woodward, Bill Wright, Woody Wright, Clorise Wynne, Wynelle, Aunt Octavia, Vivian, & Freddie Young, Reen Young, the Canaan Baptist Church family, and the GFS family Class of 2001.

A Silver Tongue is also dedicated to those loved ones we can no longer see or hold... Angels. I know they are watching over the rest of us, eternally.

In the province of the mind, what one believes to be true either is true or becomes true.

-- John Lilly

CHAPTER ONE

"My name is GB, not Gregory. You never wanted to acknowledge my real name. I am GB. That's who I am and always will be. Nobody called me Gregory before you. You're the one who started that crap."

Tuesday sat rigid, following her husband with her eyes as he paced back and forth like a caged tiger. She had no idea why he suddenly wanted to be called that name. They had been married for over seven years, and this was a first. Whew! Where'd this come from? This was strange with a capital Z. What was the big deal about his name suddenly?

When she first met him, he went by Gregory, saying he preferred it over GB, his nickname. Now here he was going on and on, ranting about his name. Why? And why today, the day they had planned a surprise party for him. Anxious, she sat holding six-year-old David in her lap, the oldest of their four children; two sets of twin boys.

"Daddy is GB, Mommy." Laughing, David turned to smile at her.

The two sat huddled in a far corner of the sofa in the family room, paying strict attention to a livid Gregory.

Holding her son, she laughed with him, tickling him under the arms. He was right; this was funny.

Already, you could see David was going to be just like his father, full of jokes.

She saw in his eyes the intelligent reflection of his father, too; his wit, his sense of humor.

One of the first things that attracted her to Gregory was his sense of humor. He always had something smart to say. And, he kept her laughing too. The other thing was his walk. Actually, he didn't walk–he strolled– like a lot of brothers in the hood. Now, even though he stood like a straight arrow, something about his posture gave way to his hoodlum past.

David saw his father's face distorted by an ugly frown.

"*Gregory*," he spit out the words, "is the person you created out of your own imagination, your damn *Sir Galahad*."

"Is Daddy mad about his name?"

Tuesday pulled her son closer, covering his ears, then released him with a hug.

"You go straight upstairs, Baby, with your brothers." His copper skin tone, and lips that made you want to kiss them, all came together to produce a likeable and handsomely boyish face. He jumped from the sofa. As he turned to take one last look, she saw the fright in her son's eyes. She puckered her lips and smiled, to let him know it was okay. He smiled gently and ran upstairs.

"Your prince? Hell no! He's your pussy-whipped king. Isn't that right? Well, it's not me! I can't live up to your dreams. I am GB! That's who I am." He said, pointing his finger, jamming it, into his chest.

Tuesday hoped their son was too far away to hear. Then she thought about the DJ in the other room, wondering if he could hear them. It shouldn't be like this, she thought. How could things have turned out this badly? She was supposed to be getting ready for a party. The smell of roasting turkey emanated from the kitchen, reminding her that it was time to baste. She checked her watch. It was almost six o'clock. Who would think that a simple party would cause this much commotion?

Gregory quieted.

She thought back to earlier that same afternoon.

The plans Gregory made should have kept him out of the house for hours, at least 'til eight or nine. While he was gone she'd started cooking and decorating. To her shock, he'd returned early.

"Surprise!" she said, nearly falling off the stepladder as Gregory walked through the front door, she remembered. To celebrate the end of his air traffic controller's training at the Airport, Tuesday had decided to surprise him with a party. All of his friends and family were invited–including Griffin, one of Gregory's oldest homeboys, who lived two hours away. Cleverly, she kept the party a surprise, changing the subject whenever he walked in on her if she happened to be on the phone discussing it. Surreptitiously, she made all the arrangements while he was at work. The only glitch was that she hadn't known how to keep him away from the house until all the party people arrived; nor did she know how to get him back if he had gone out alone. He worked such strange hours and didn't have a lot of friends. Oh well, she rationalized; a surprise party is still a surprise no matter when the person finds out about it, right? She looked down at him, smiling, a little embarrassed.

Gregory was not amused. "Another party? Who's party this time?"

"It's for you, silly. Who else?"

Gregory decided he'd heard enough and started toward the stairs. He'd seen the decorations from his car when he pulled into the driveway. The thought had crossed his mind to just turn around and go somewhere else. The only reason he decided to come in was because he'd been out the night before, and he was tired. He stopped on the stairs, hesitating. It would serve her right to have to greet all of her so-called guests by herself. They were all a bunch of freeloaders as far as he was concerned. What was this party all about, anyway? The more he thought about it, the angrier he became. I should turn around and leave. Didn't she throw a birthday party for Duce and Gabriel just a few weeks ago?

He wanted to say something. He felt like telling her about herself, about everything he knew about her sneakin' around, but figured it wasn't worth it right now, deciding instead to go on up to their room.

Tuesday almost lost her balance again on the ladder. What is he mad about now? she wondered. Steadying herself, she watched him, then shook her head and went back to the decorations. He seemed angry about everything, she thought as she pinned the streamer to the wall.

The telephone started to ring. She let it ring about three times looking at the ceiling. Exasperated, she climbed down the ladder to answer it on the sixth ring.

"Hey, Tuesday. Aisha wanted to know what time we should come. She lost the invitation." It was Jerry Cunningham. He always seemed to be out of breath, as though he were running and talking at the same time. He and his wife lived a few blocks away.

"Jerry, I'm telling you now, you need refrigerator magnets. You may as well get used to it. All important notes go there, on the fridge. Tell Aisha for me, too. Now that you have a three-year old daughter, it's the only way to keep track of things, like parties, parent-teacher meetings, doctor appointments and everything else."

"Hold on, Jerry. Someone's at the door."

Opening the door, hot air had rushed in, stinging her face. The DJ stood out there with more music and equipment than she would have ever imagined was needed for one party.

"Come in," she breathed. He looked like a one-man band. "I'm on the phone, but you can start bringing your stuff in." Turning, she ran back to the phone.

"Nine o'clock is good, Jerry. Okay? See you then," she said.

After showing the DJ where to set up, she went back to the decorations.

Upstairs, Gregory laid down on the bed fully-dressed with the covers pulled over him. He was lying in the fetal position. Even with all his clothes on and the covers over him, he was still feeling cold and jittery. He had been bothered all day, knowing she was doing something behind his back. He lay thinking, trying to calm down, when he heard Tuesday coming up the stairs. *Now what*, he thought.

She stood in the doorway. "Are you okay, Sweetheart?"

Not bothering to look at her, he turned over and stared at the bedroom ceiling.

"Come on. Get up. *Please.*"

Gregory looked past her toward the stairs. They could hear the children playing in their rooms and the DJ moving around on the first floor. "Come on. Please."

"Listen, I'm outta here!" Fuming, he looked at her as though she had kicked him. He jumped up out of the bed and stalked past her, out of the room.

"What is it? Are you upset about the party? Talk to me, please. Greg. What is happening here?" Tuesday followed him downstairs trying to get a handle on why he was so angry. A laughing David had slid down the banister behind them, plopping himself into his mother's lap.

She'd sent him back upstairs, and now, here they were.

"I told you, my name is GB, not Greg."

Pacing back and forth, he glared at her. What does she think she's doin'? The last thing he wanted was to entertain a bunch of people. Gregory stopped to reach for his glass. A feeling of dread had been lurking in his head for some time now, skulking around, searching. The little booger was like a dirty little trash picker, singling out long-forgotten memories; tossing them aside, only to lift another scrap from a corner of his mind and examine it, too. At times, Gregory could see its face, lips twisted in pure disgust. In the past, he'd only seen it and felt it; today it spoke directly to him.

"*Look at that smile; you sucker. You probably think that phony, little, innocent smile means she wasn't screwing somebody's brains out both nights while you were away? Somebody like her 'buddy' from the law firm at work? Hell, she doesn't even have to wait 'til night. They can screw around all day long. She can come home and just show you those pearly whites and say, 'I had to work late,' in that phony-baloney innocent little voice. And you, you dumb-ass, pussy-whipped motherfucker, you believe it,*" it said, mockingly laughing at him.

Gregory tried not to listen. He didn't want to believe what he was hearing, but his gut overrode his conscious mind. It reminded him of the troubled feeling he'd had that other time, just last month. He'd gone to work, as usual. The drive across the airfield to the radar room gave no indication of the events to come. His crew chief held a de-briefing, as usual, and he'd taken his place in front of the radar screen.

As usual, little blips with transponder information attached to them were scattered across his screen.

He gave an instruction to one aircraft pilot after another, letting them know he was there, and in charge of things. Everything seemed to be going smoothly. Relaxing, he directed GTX 8490 to turn dogleg and begin his descent for landing.

"Roger, okay, tower," the pilot answered. After a few moments Greg noted that the aircraft was still at the same altitude. Scratching his head, something instinctive made him ask the pilot to check it out. "GTX 8490, say altitude. Over."

"Roger approach. GTX 8490 is at one seven thousand."

Come to find out, the altimeter reading was wrong. GTX 8490's transponder was giving out erroneous information. If he hadn't caught it who knows what could have happened?

"Told you so," said the voice only Gregory could hear.

It spoke once more. *"This little party is just a cover-up. She's planning to hat up, Jack, any day now. She's going to do a little disappearing act on your dumb ass. She's going to make like a tree and leave. She's going to make like a banana and split once this is over,"* the little voice said, making utter and complete sense.

Gregory nodded. That's it, he agreed, a diversion tactic. He'd heard her, sneaking around, whispering on the phone, changin' the conversation when he came in the room. What had he been thinking? Yeah, that was it. *That* was the plan! He could see it clearly now, thinking back to a few weeks ago, visualizing her reaction to the news that he had to go away for a two-day conference. She'd just pretended to be upset: That she didn't want him to go. Tuesday was a very good actress. She probably had somebody on the side, too, he persuaded himself.

"I told you, I haven't been promoted and I don't want a party. I told you before; we're going down the tubes. We're broke."

Tuesday, hearing a dark, hollow sound, thought someone else was in the room with them. Convinced, she turned to look.

Realizing it was Gregory answering her question, she turned back, astonished.

"Why do you keep saying we're broke? When I was in law school and didn't have a steady income, we were fine, financially. Now I've passed the bar, I'm working and you've gotten a raise. We have a lot more money than before. But you say we're broke, Gregory. I don't understand."

"Look at her," dread spit out the sickening words, having gained its own nasty little voice.

"Look at her," the feeling persisted, *"she acts like butter wouldn't melt in her mouth, like she's motherfucking Earth-Mother or somebody."*

"You," Gregory hissed, pointing an accusing finger at her, "don't understand. You still think you can fool me, don't you? You think the world revolves around you and everything you want. Well, listen here!" His voice started to rise slightly.

"It doesn't." Taking control, he glanced toward the dining room. Tuesday followed his eyes. They stood silent, before she spoke.

"What're you saying? I should call off the party? Or should I call you GB from now on? What?"

"What do you think I'm saying?"

"That's it! Good. Keep her off balance. Mess with her head the way she's messing with your head, trying to keep you on a string until she's good and ready. Then she'll cut you loose without so much as a see-you-later-sucker. Just remember, keep your cool."

She made a little laughing sound. "I'm just trying to make sense of what you're saying here. I was only trying to give you a surprise party. Now, what's wrong with that?"

Just then the thought occurred to her that maybe he was still feeling the shame of the forced demotion and transfer from his job at the International Airport the year before. That maybe he still felt the sting of it, and now he was taking those feelings out on her. She softened. She could never mention it for obvious reasons, but also because she understood how he felt.

Then she stood, all five feet two of her.

Gregory was seething. "I-have-not-been-promoted-and-I-do-not-want-to-have-a-promotion-party."

"Well then… let's just spend some time with our friends," Tuesday soothed.

"Okay?" She started toward him, but changed her mind. "Are you okay, Sweetheart?" Concerned, she stared at her husband.

Then, glancing at her watch, Tuesday said, "Baby. Sweetheart. I'm trying to understand how you're feeling, but; I'm a little confused about all this. Is there any way we can talk about this later, Babe? It's getting late, and I need to take the boys to my parents."

He looked at her then at the doorway. They were silent again, as the only noise was the hum of the window air-conditioner, giving off a steady flow of cool air, and the DJ moving in the dining room, setting up his music.

She reached out again, this time laying a quieting hand on his upper arm.

"Okay? Please?" Brightening her tone, Tuesday pulled at her tee shirt.

"Come on. Relax. Look at me. I've still got to change and get the kids settled. And put the food out. Now that you know about it, you can help."

She laughed. "We've got a party to get ready for." She reached for his hand.

He pulled away. "Listen, I'm outta here," he said, walking with his back turned to her.

Tuesday followed.

"What is it? Talk to me. Please, Greg, what's happening here?"

He stopped at the front door, about to leave her alone to greet their impending guests, as an Audi 100 pulled up in front of their house. They both looked on as the strangely unfamiliar car quieted, and the door opened.

"You can have all the parties you want, but I'm outta here," Gregory said over his shoulder. He opened the door and stepped out onto the porch.

Just then the driver unbuckled his seatbelt and turned to stretch his legs outside the car.

Tuesday was losing ground. The screen door separated them. Quickly, she tried to figure out what to say so that Gregory wouldn't leave, when at last he recognized the New York license plates.

Larry jumped out of the car and quickly strolled over to greet his older brother. He was part of the surprise.

"Grea-a-a-t day. Larry! What are you doin' here?" Gregory hugged his brother tight. Laughing, he asked, "Man, did you know about this party?"

"Yeah. Of course, I knew about it. That's why I'm here." Larry slapped his brother on the shoulder.

"Help me with these bags, GB," Larry said walking back to the car. He pulled his luggage from the trunk of the Audi.

"That was a long-ass drive, Dude. Took me seven hours to get to Philly, Man."

Larry let out an exhausted breath and greeted Tuesday. "How you doin' girl, with your fine brown self?"

They hadn't seen each other in a long while, and hugged one another tightly.

She whispered. "Just in time, Baby Brother. Thanks."

Gregory was happy to see his brother, having come all the way from Rochester.

"Drove all the way just for my party?" Gregory had an ear-to-ear smile.

"Man, it's good to see you. Stand back, let me take a look." Larry was a few inches taller than his brother and had a little less melanin in his skin; still they shared a strong family resemblance.

Although Larry was only a few years younger, they had a paternalistic relationship, nonetheless. From the time he was seventeen years old and joined the Air Force, Gregory had helped to supplement his family's income by sending his parents almost half of his paltry serviceman's pay: at first for GP, then to help Larry, and then to help his sister get through college. Now, Larry was on his feet and apparently doing well.

Gregory had also hit the big time; earning a good living as a civilian Air Traffic Controller with a wife who was giving him a surprise promotion, or 'whatever' party.

"Alright. Man you must be working out. You doin' alright for yourself," he admired, laughing at the same time. "Look at this car, Tue.

"Man… where you working, again? You still in marketing and sales? You must be pulling down the ducketts for real." Gregory slapped his brother a high five.

Laughing, Gregory made a complete about-face, as he seemingly forgot about the previous situation just five minutes prior, acting as if nothing had been wrong only minutes before.

Tuesday watched in amazement as he laughed out loud.

He and Larry jabbered away at a mile a minute. Gregory, remembering his wife, smiled broadly at her. "I'm gonna take Larry and his bags upstairs, Tue."

Tuesday smiled, following them back into the house, where she then gathered all four boys and their overnight bags. Happy to have things back to normal, she gave instructions to the DJ before leaving to drop the older set of twins, David and Daniel, at the babysitter's and getting the youngest set of twins, Gregory and Gabriel, to her parent's house.

PTER TWO

the door flew open. Jerry and
se announcing, "*the party has now*

m, slapping Jerry a high five.
and Derrick Spielberg, who had
understood the announcement
was time to eat, and walked briskly to the buffet
table. They knew the most delectable foods were on
display, so neither stopped to say much of anything to
anyone. They went straight to the dimly-lit dining room, a
large area 30 by 30 feet, about the size of a small ballroom.
The newly-painted walls were a deep forest green, bordered
by a sophisticated pink and green pattern. The space was
pulled together and made rich by a shiny gold leaf chair rail
trim all around. Gold-plated sconces hung flush against the
walls, used to accent original framed artwork. A bejeweled,
multicolored Tiffany chandelier hung from the ceiling
overlooking an antique solid oak dining table with an inlaid
veneer pattern, sculpted legs and matching chairs. The
effect was magical.

Tuesday noticed the two and stopped them to chat.
"I hope you two are enjoying yourselves."

"We certainly are, Tuesday. I could smell this food
a mile away, all the way over to my house. You know,

Derrick and I always try to be the first ones at your parties, to make sure we get some of everything." Nancy sampled a little of each, talking too, as she made her way around the table.

"Hmmm... This stuffed bluefish with the dill cream sauce is scrumptious. Is this stuffed with crab and shrimp?" She took another forkful of food. "Hmmm... You go, Girl. And these collard greens—they just melt in your mouth.

"Look at this spread; I think I've died and gone to Heaven," she said with her arms outstretched.

"Mounds of fried chicken, crispy, golden. How'd you do that? And over here, these barbecued ribs are bangin'. And I haven't even gotten to the roast beef and the turkey yet. You couldn't have cooked all this food by yourself."

Derrick finished filling his plate and went to sit down.

Gregory and Tuesday's friends were in unanimous agreement when it came to her culinary skills. They agreed she was an exceptionally-talented cook and entertained her guests well. Tuesday had enrolled in gourmet cooking classes here and there over the years and always set out a lavish spread. But tonight, now that she was working and had four kids to raise; she had the help of a caterer.

"No way could I do all this by myself, but you know I had to cook something. And my mother always has to make her potato salad."

"Well, I'm glad she did because I know it's delicious. Let me get a little right now." She added a spoonful to her plate.

"Oh my God! Tuesday, this looks like the creamiest baked macaroni and cheese ever. And those anchovies seem to be swimming in that Caesar salad over there. And what's this?"

Tuesday laughed. "Calm down, Nancy. This is the caterer's special ambrosia."

"Special?"

"Well, he says he uses only the freshest and sweetest fruits available in season, and that he has a secret ingredient in his sauce. He says it's an aphrodisiac."

They chuckle.

"I'll have to make sure Derrick and I eat a lot of that, then." They finished making their way around the table.

"Be sure to watch out for the fireworks, later over the dessert. He made a Baked Alaska, and he's going to fire up some Cherries Jubilee to be served over homemade ice cream. And don't forget to taste my grandmother's candy-crusted sweet potato pie."

"Oh my God! I *have* died and gone right to Heaven right here in your house, Tuesday. Wait 'til I tell Derrick." She pointed with her fork. "Is that Greg's brother over there?"

Tuesday nodded. "I'm glad he was able to make it to the party. Maybe he'll meet somebody he likes and he'll move here, to East Oak Lane, near us. What do you think? Sound like a plan?"

"Sounds like a plan to me. Too bad I'm not eligible. Don't think Derrick would take to the idea of his moving in with us. He sure looks good, though. How old is he now?"

"Ah… Larry must be twenty-five now. He's four years younger than us. And what are you doin' lookin' at him anyway, Missy?" She nodded toward Derrick. "I thought you preferred blonde-haired, blue-eyed men."

"Hey, just because I married one doesn't mean I can't admire a brother." They laughed.

Derrick came over, plate in hand. "Tuesday, those ribs were smack-yo-momma-good. I gotta get some more of those. Hey, girls. What's so funny?"

"Nothing, Hon, I'll tell you later." Nancy winked at Tuesday.

The party was starting to pick up. Everybody showed through. Millie, a perfect size eight, made an entrance, appearing in an ankle-length dress so tight you could hear her bellybutton scream. If it weren't for the sheer black netting that covered her shoulders and arms, Millie would have been entirely naked along the top, but the diaphanous material actually made the look sophisticated and sexy. The satin ribbon added just the right touch of glamour, the way it rose from the mounds of her behind, traveling upward, caressing her waist in passing, to cross one breast; and then wound its way around her neck. From there it headed down to criss-cross the other breast; completing the journey where it began; at the bottom of her completely exposed flawless back. The dress was black-on-black, in black. It fit like a glove.

"*Millie*." Tuesday hugged her friend tight. "Girl… that dress is the bomb. It is so sharp. Now you know you're goin' to make every woman in here jealous. You wear that just to cause trouble, Girlfriend?" They giggled.

"Yo, Tuesday. Who's your friend?"

Millie and Tuesday looked around to face Jerry, standing with two drinks, one in each hand. "Oh, Jerry. You remember Millie, don't you?"

"Oh, yeah. Millie," said Jerry smiling. "Hey, I didn't recognize you in that dress. You about to hurt a brotha in that dress, Girl. How you doin'?"

"Hi, Jerry. How've you been? And Aisha, right?" She gave him a peck on the cheek.

"Yeah. Aisha. I was just getting' us a little something," he said hurriedly. His hands were full, carrying a plate and drinks.

"When you get a chance, stop over. We're over there," he motioned with his elbow.

"Okay Jerry," Tuesday said, taking over. "I see the Blacksmiths, Jackie and Bruce, and I want to take Millie over to meet them. She'll be free to talk to you later. I promise."

"Jackie Blacksmith is here? The physician? Where?" Jerry asked, surprised.

Tuesday nodded her head in the direction of the couple. "You know her? Did you two go to medical school together?"

"I know her from high school. We went to Willingboro High together. I gotta go say hi to her. Hey, I didn't know you knew her, too."

"I met her when I was pregnant with my youngest twins, about six years ago. She's a very good doctor, you know."

"Hey, well tell her to save me a dance." He seemed to get somewhat anxious, and added. "I better take this drink over to Aisha before she comes lookin' for me. Tell Jackie I'll get over to her before the night is out."

Millie and Tuesday joined the Blacksmiths.

As the party spilled outside into the warm June night, the four of them followed the crowd out the side door, talking as they went.

As they took turns chatting, Tuesday took a mental survey of things. The caterer had done a good job of decorating outside. Tables were decked out with various richly-colored tablecloths. On each table was a vase, which held bright blue flowers. Japanese lanterns hung overhead, their glow glistening and shimmering off the water where people surrounded the heated pool. The light fragrance of citronella candles set upright on bamboo stalks was carried throughout by a sensual, gentle wind whispering across the freshly cut backyard lawn. Smiling, she felt satisfied that everyone was having a good time. A perfect summer night, she thought.

"Looks like all the good ones are taken," said Millie after the Blacksmiths had gone off to dance.

"Oh?   Are you looking for another husband, already?"

"No way. At least, not yet," Millie laughed. She'd come purposely without a date; happy to be single again.

"I'm just here to have a good time. If I meet somebody… well, let's just leave it at that. I'm ready to dance, that's all."

Even though six months had passed since her divorce, she wanted to party like it was 1999, again. When she moved her hips, everyone noticed. The unattached men lined up, waiting their turn for a dance with her, hoping to get a glimpse of her café-au-lait thighs when the long split at either side of her dress permitted. A few of the more savvy wives allowed their husbands to dance with her, too, knowing their men would get worked up. The wives counted on it, for later, when they were back home in bed.

Bruce Blacksmith stood alone at the bar watching.

Tuesday had gone to speak with the caterer, to thank him for the extra touches he'd added to the decor. She finished, and was about to start looking for Greg when she heard it. A wisp of wind carrying with it the far off sound of laughter and singing, made her think her younger brother, Adam, and his crew were on the way. After a moment, she was sure that it was him--because she could hear trumpets and whistles blowing and getting closer. She heard jangling tambourines and people singing at the top of their lungs. It could be no one other than him, she thought, because Adam and his personal entourage always arrived in a flourish.

He'd asked if he could bring some friends along, but from the sound of it, he must have several carloads with him this time, she thought again. Sighing, she let out a small, embarrassed laugh. Tuesday braced herself and worked her way back into the house so she could greet him at the door and check out his clique.

She didn't know who he might be with tonight. On the one hand, he hung out with an elite set of up and coming movers and shakers, mostly young black attorneys like himself. On the other hand, he could be seen cavorting with some of the most unsavory ghetto characters you'd ever want to meet; some clients, some friends, one could never guess which. Lately, he seemed to be on a personal mission where the end goal was self-destruction. Getting into trouble with drugs in high school remarkably, he'd made it straight through college, graduating from law school in record time at age twenty-two. But after that he seemed determined to destroy himself, delving further into the drug culture. She and her parents thought that her brother was just going through a phase, but now, five years later, it seems to be a permanent part of his makeup. She still loved her brother, but had little patience for him. He had been invited even though they had grown apart after the baby died, she and he going their separate ways, only coming together for family outings or gatherings such as this.

The music from the car radios silenced. She heard several car doors being slammed shut. Standing there in the doorway she was able to pick him out from the crowd, which was moving toward her. Amused, she watched as he came closer. He always seemed to be dancing, The Bopper, they called him. She smiled. As he came into full view, she caught a glimpse of him. Lord, was he handsome, and always dressed to kill, reminding her of a modern day Duke Ellington. She frowned. She could see why he stayed in so much trouble with the ladies, always smiling, always gracious, always dancing. Greeting him with a hug, she smiled politely as he and his friends made their way through the door, mixing into the crowd.

People arrived in a steady stream, which kept the party fresh.

The DJ played a mix of old school and new, the kind of music that'll bring out the party in anyone, full force.

"Take the roof off the sucker," Jerry chanted, eyeing his wife, who pranced from side to side, laughing. A look of concern suddenly covered his face. He held his wife by the arm.

"Don't look now, but Adam just walked in."

Aisha turned, slightly, seeing him from the corner of her eye.

"You want to go?"

"No, I'm okay. I'm not going to let him ruin my night out," she feigned a laugh.

"Finally. I found you. Come on. Let's dance." Across the room, Gregory clutched Tuesday around her waist and pulled her close as *Love*, from Musiq Soulchild's CD started.

"Thanks for the party, Babe. I'm sorry I was such a pain earlier," he whispered close into her ear. Continuing to move rhythmically across the floor, their bodies moved as one, grasping one another by interlocking fingers, he placed a free hand firmly into the small of her back, and led the way.

She liked the way the he held her, giving her a feeling of security, she relaxed, molding herself to fit perfectly within his tight grip.

"That's okay. I have to admit though; you had me scared for a little while there. I didn't know what was going on. But, I'm glad everything turned out all right." Throwing her head back in a laugh, she looked up at him, giving him a quick kiss and a wink.

"There was one more surprise, though."

"Look up this way. Smile for the camera," the photographer clicked. "Okay, one mo' time. And this time give me lotsa teeth."

Tuesday did as told, grinning foolishly into the camera, feeling her husband's hard body next to hers. The camera's lights flashed.

Gregory smiled wide, then, closed his mouth slightly. He didn't want the camera to pick up on his gold tooth. It was pretty far back in his mouth, but in pictures it appeared to be an empty space, as if one of his teeth were missing. So, he always remembered not to smile too brightly for the camera. Friends teased him about it. Tuesday said he should get it removed, but he liked having something of his past as a reminder of how far he'd come.

Another flash went off in their eyes.

"Okay, folks. I think I shot just about e'erbody here. I'm goin' out to my van, process this here film, and I'll be right back so e'erbody can see their pictures." He moved to leave.

"I hope you didn't forget to take one of my brother and his car," Gregory reminded.

The photographer stopped and turned.

"Nope. I got it right here." He patted his camera bag and sped off.

As another tune began, they laughed and went back to mold themselves into a dance as soulful as only the unique voice of Jill Scott could make it.

Tuesday nuzzled her face into his chest.

"Where were we? Oh. I was telling you about the last surprise. It doesn't look like it's going to work out, though."

"No? What was it?"

"Griffin. I finally got his number, last week, and told him about the party. He said he would be here. I know it would have meant a lot to you, and I was looking forward to seeing him, too."

"Griffin was the surprise? Cool," Gregory nodded and kissed the top of her head. "It's late, but maybe he'll still show.

"By the way, I got a whiff of your grandmother's sweet potato pie a while ago. Did you make sure to put at least one pie away for us?"

"Oh yeah. You know it, Sweetie."

"Okay, I just wanted to make sure I got some. Larry, too."

Everyone, it seemed, had been transformed, as one and all the partygoers danced to the never-ending sounds. The DJ heated things up with Mary J, *Not Gon' Cry*, while Will kept everyone on the dance floor *Gettin' Jiggy Wit It* until small rays of sunlight glimmered through the dark sky.

"Well, I'm going straight to bed, you two. It was a long drive, but the party was worth it. Congratulations, bro. Good job, Tue." Larry kissed her on the cheek and headed up the stairs.

Not long after they had shown the last guest to the door, the two made their way up and lay quiet in bed. The darkened room was large-scale, like all the rooms in their house. A ceiling fan hummed overhead, lulling the two into a dreamy hypnotic state. The stress of the day's activities had left Gregory with an insatiable void. Wordlessly, his large hand reached out and moved indelicately over the smooth skin of Tuesday's small breasts. He meant to take her at this moment, no questions asked, he pulled her close.

After more than seven years of marriage, Gregory had long ago made her understand that in this regard he would not take no for an answer. Bending her to his will, he used the tips of his fingers to twist her skin and tug at her, sadistically guiding her this way, and that.

She knew what he wanted, pressing hard against her, it nuzzled hugely against her back, growing thicker and stiffer as his hands searched and pinched her body in a fierce caress.

"Give it to me, Tue. You know I'm gonna take it anyway."

Pulling her hair with one hand, he turned her head and forced her mouth to his, urgently discovering every corner with his tongue; as if he might devour her, reminding her that she belonged to him.

She relented, feeling the veins of his hardness through the silkiness of her panties, as though there were nothing separating him from her.

Releasing her for the moment, his arms came around each side of her waist. Pulling her ever more closely he placed both of his warm hands inside her panties, removing them, he found her small and soft. One huge finger slid along the lips of the tender opening between her legs. As he massaged her with the palm of his hand, a warm feeling spread along her thighs.

She knew there would be pain, yet she yearned to feel him inside her. She was repulsed by his rough foreplay, but knew it was better to let him have his way. Her entire body silently urged him on.

He jammed three fingers inside of her.

She let out a small noise.

Again, he pressed against her, his fingers probing, sliding in and out.

Then, turning her over, he slid toward the foot of the bed, at the same time using his fingers to lift her and guide her tenderness to his waiting mouth. Within minutes the soft touch of his lips burrowed between her legs, forcing her hips to press into his face.

He used his tongue to alternately massage her, coaxing her juices to him, then to suck hard, determined to milk every possible drop from her.

An anguished moan escaped her.

Her body stimulated to the point of no return, she began writhing furiously as Gregory seemingly sapped her dry.

Suddenly he raised up, taking her, the two joined in continual motion, pleasuring one another until finally, they lay exhausted and out of breath; content to drift in and out of sleeplessness. They dozed.

But, the hunger within Gregory roared too loudly, too angrily, to allow for the peace required of slumber.

"Tue. I'm sorry, but I need you. Now." Wanting more, he squeezed her nipples until they were swollen and painful, then used his tongue to gently soothe them.

While the area between her legs still contracted and throbbed, Gregory slipped a moist finger into her, and then another, and another. She gasped, knowing he was readying her for what was to come next.

Molding her into position, he began to squeeze the tip of his manhood into the smallest of openings.

This time, she let out a scream of pain and terror. She took deep breaths. Then, relaxing her muscles to accommodate the huge, pulsing presence within her, she let her mind go blank as he continued to push deeper.

He pushed harder and deeper and faster until he made one final, long, powerful drive, calling her name.

From behind, he moaned, "Tuesday, I love you."

Again, her body shook, deliriously filled with a combination of pain and delight.

Finished, he cradled her like a limp doll in his arms, holding her tightly.

"I love you more than you'll ever know, Tue.

"Please tell me if doing it this way is too much for you."

She started to say something, but he continued.

"I know you said it's okay, but the way you scream every time, makes me think I'm killing you."

"It's alright, Sweetheart. It hurts initially, but after a while it's really okay. I'll do anything for you. I love you." She kissed him gently.

They got up and showered together.

In the shower he soaped her back gently. Knowing the pain he caused, he determined to use his tongue to make up for it under the running water.

This time languidly massaging her as the warmth of the water caressed her skin, he kissed her neck and shoulders. Continuing, he kissed her body, her breasts, down her thighs, giving her time, coaxing, urging, until once again she drifted in a gentle rolling wave of sheer ecstasy.

Once again, her buttery sweetness and sounds of joy caused him to become erect. Dripping wet, carrying her to the bed, once again he mounted her.

CHAPTER THREE

Larry woke the next day to sunshine and blue skies and the smell of freshly-baked Danish. He liked that, and wondered who was downstairs doing the cooking. Rising up to rest himself on his elbows, he thought, most likely it was Tuesday, but it could have been GB. Both he and his brother were pretty good cooks. That was one thing their mother had insisted on teaching them—how to cook and how to clean up after themselves. She had determined that they be independent and (at the very least) she wanted to make sure they wouldn't be a burden to any woman. Still, Larry enjoyed being catered to. He loved days like today, where all he had to do was wake up and go downstairs to breakfast. A warm house, family, someone to talk to in the mornings; there was nothing like it as far as he was concerned. Right now all he had was a cat, one who liked to hang out in the streets more than he did. His brother was living the life. A nice wife, four great kids... well, two sets of twins was a bit much, but at least they had enough room in this big house. So, that made it okay. And the house. How much did a place like this cost? Musta been an arm and a leg. Just look at the size of this bedroom. He scanned the room quickly. It was huge. Enormous.

Did Greg say it was a Victorian? Forty-two windows, eleven gigantic rooms, three fireplaces, two balconies and a back stairway. Tuesday told him the history of the house. She'd said the servants used it to travel from one floor to the next. In researching the history of the house, she'd also discovered information about the abolitionists who used to live here and the part they played in the Underground Railroad. The back stairway was also used to sneak run-away slaves up to the secret rooms on the second floor. From here in Philadelphia, the newly freed would make their way to the next stop, which was Lancaster, Pennsylvania; then finally, on to Canada.

Hearing a noise, he got up and went to the closet thinking he'd find one of his nephews hiding there. Seeing no one, he fished out the robe he'd put there the day before. Then he remembered that the boys had spent the night elsewhere. Closing the door, he turned away.

Again, he heard a rustling sound. This time he quickly opened the door, laughing. Greg must be trying to pull a fast one, he thought. Looking through his clothes hanging in the closet he spotted the secret entrance, a small door, which was usually hidden from view by the clothing stored there. That's right, he thought, remembering the house's background. He'd said they would sneak run-away slaves up and into one of the two tiny concealed rooms hidden in-between the walls. But what was that noise? He bent to get a better look.

The door was so small a modern six-year-old would have to stoop to get through. His brother told him that it had been cut out of the far wall of the closet. And, that the room opposite this closet had been made smaller by the two-feet, which the hiding place required. He noted the latch on the diminutive door, and realized that it could only be opened from the outside; locking automatically once the door was closed. Providing a level of security for the hosts, no doubt. Once a person went into the space, they were in, until someone undid the latch from the outside.

He smiled, remembering the story of his twin nephews, David and Daniel, the older twins, and how they had discovered the small places. They'd decided to use them as perfect hiding spaces in a game of hide-and-seek. Once, though, they'd locked themselves in and had to wait, banging and screaming, for what they said seemed like hours, before their mother, Tuesday, found them and finally opened the tiny elf-sized door.

Still, what about that noise? He could have sworn it came from inside the closet. Opening the door, he crawled inside to see if maybe an animal had gotten up in there. What he saw was an empty space. And the fragrance of hot buttered Danish and sweet potato pie was now replaced by a hundred year-old dusty odor. Obviously, the meager guest quarters had been built to accommodate no more than two or three cramped adult bodies at a time; he could see that. But he was sure the run-away slave did not mind, and would hide there no matter what the circumstances, locked in the narrow space until it was time to move on to the next stop on the road to freedom. There was nothing more to see. The space was empty.

Dismissing the thought, Larry crawled out, closing the door as he went. Going into the bathroom, he began to brush his teeth. A mental picture of Millie and the party last night came to him. Now there was somebody to wake up to. She was good-looking, true enough, but what turned him on most was her conversation. She was smart, had it goin' on upstairs. Being a professional psychologist was a little unnerving, in that he couldn't be sure she wasn't playing head games with him. But, she seemed sincere. Whatever. He was going to add her to his *to-do* list, and call her today. Larry showered and shaved while thinking about what strategy to use. He was drying off when the idea hit him. He knew just what to say. If there was anything happening, he'd find out. If she wasn't interested, he'd find that out, too; all without seeming obvious and without losing face. He smiled as he dressed. Then, congratulated himself on using his skill as a marketing rep to help him become a true player. Thinking about which special move he was going to make, he made his way down to breakfast.

Millie stared at her reflection in the bathroom mirror, toothbrush poised in her open mouth. What was she staring at? Why had she stopped brushing her teeth? Then she remembered. Larry. Greg's younger brother. They'd danced most of the night, then talked 'til daybreak. He was sweet, but was she ready for another serious relationship? Not just yet. She'd had a good time with him last night. And as long as they could keep it that way, fine. But, another face kept popping up from last night, too. And this one, she knew, she had no business thinking about.

Bruce turned his head to look at Jackie, wondering about the two of them. She lay sound asleep beside him. As was his habit, he watched her breathe. How long had it been now? Sixteen years? Almost half his life, he'd been married to the same person. Nowadays that was the same as forever. He loved everything about her and couldn't get enough of her at times, like now. At thirty-four, she seemed to be blossoming. Her face so content. Beautiful.

He touched her chin and kissed her gently. Through the soft cotton sheet he could make out the shape of her breasts. He was filled with wanting to hold her, and soon he became aroused. Reaching out, he stroked her nipple through the sheet. She opened her eyes and smiled up at him.

Jerry decided to get up early and go for a run. He wanted to be out of the house before Aisha awoke. He didn't feel like answering her jealous-filled questions this morning. He grabbed a pair of shorts and threw on a tee-shirt. Carrying his socks and sneakers, he stole quietly down the stairs and out through the gate. He started out in a measured gait, disappearing down the street and around the corner.

Aisha was in the kitchen when he returned, hot and sweaty. The aroma of bacon and coffee greeted him at the door.

"Good morning," he said grabbing a towel from the powder room.

"Morning to you, too." She barely looked up.

"You sleep alright?" he used quick movements drying himself of sweat on his forearms and neck.

"Yeah. Right through your snoring. You know you snore whenever you drink. You know that, right?"

"I know. Hey, you told me before. I'm sorry. Okay?"

"You want something to eat? I cooked." She poured herself and then him a cup of coffee.

"I see. Smells good, too."

"Well?"

"Oh. Yeah. Hey. I wanna eat. Thanks."

She made two plates and set them on the table.

"Well. What did you think about the party last night? And what about Adam? Hey, can you believe that guy?" He slapped his thighs with both hands and rubbed them in a rushing motion.

"Adam is a fool. I hate him for what he did to my sister. And for the baby, too, for Angel."

"When was the last time you heard from Rasheeda?"

"She wrote to me last week, but I haven't had a chance to write back yet. I wish I could go visit her more often. But, you know…" She trailed off.

"Why do they build prisons so far away from the city, when they say most of the prisoners are black and from the inner cities? Makes no sense. And him being a lawyer, couldn't help her get a break. I hate that bastard. The only reason I put up with him is because of Tuesday. At least she tried to help Rasheeda."

He touched her hand, trying to comfort his wife. "I know what you mean. It's hard to believe they're related to each other. They're so different. He seems to think everything is fun and games. Did he ever get his law license back?"

"I don't know, but I hope he never does. That bastard. I'll never forgive him for turning my sister out on crack the way he did. And if it weren't for Tuesday… I don't know what I would have done when Angel died."

Jerry stroked her.

They sipped the rest of their coffee in silence.

CHAPTER FOUR

Ever since the day of the party she'd noticed it. It had only been a few weeks, but something was different. She couldn't put her finger on it, but it was there, the change was real. Lately, it seemed that the slightest thing aggravated him and triggered an avalanche of name calling and cursing. So, when Gregory asked, "Did anything special happen today?" she eyed him suspiciously.

They were seated at the dining room table when he asked the question, and just then, the lights dimmed, then brightened again. Everyone, including the boys, stared up at the chandelier.

"Looks like they're at it again," Tuesday laughed weakly.

"Did our ghost do that, Daddy?" asked one of the kids.

Gregory reached for his water glass. "Uh huh. Eat your food."

She continued to stare upward, trying to buy time, knowing her answer to his question could mean the difference between a quiet evening at home reading, talking, laughing or; one spent in hell with a ranting, raving maniac. What was a girl to do? She analyzed his body language and decided that, for the moment he seemed fine and that maybe, just maybe, it was okay to answer honestly.

"What the hell is she looking at? What fuckin' lie is she tryin' to make up now?" The little voice asked Gregory.

"Well," Tuesday hesitated.

"I'm excited about one of my new cases. It could mean a big bonus if I win. But, you know how that goes." She raised her fork to her mouth and looked at Gregory, waiting for a comment.

He said nothing.

"Here we go again. Work. Work. Work. That's all she can think about. And you know why, right? Of course you do. Because you know who's there, at the office. The one she fucks around with all day. And I don't mean that figuratively, either."

Steadily, she became more uncomfortable, feeling she'd made a mistake, but dared not show a sign. She looked away, still holding her fork, continuing to make light conversation.

"Mm-hmm. Let the dumb bitch keep running her mouth. She'll put her foot in it soon. The stupid, dumb sow can't help it. She doesn't care about you nor the boys or this house or nothin' if it doesn't have to do with her and what she calls 'work'."

"Of course, it'll be a long time before anything can come of it. We'll probably need to try the case. And you know how long something like that can take." She put her fork down on her plate. Her mouth dry, she took a sip from her glass and gulped hard enough to hurt her throat.

Forcing a smile, she continued. "And there's another case up for grabs. It's actually quite interesting; where an attorney, now disbarred, was indicted, along with an accountant I met at a networking function just a few months ago. They're both accused of conspiracy, trying to bilk the estate of a dead man, a cousin of the lawyer. Supposedly, they embezzled the estate out of $1.5 million dollars."

Pausing, she gazed at her husband.

Still, Gregory said nothing.

Nervous, but steady, she continued.

"Our firm is representing the attorney, for whatever good it'll do. Can you believe it?"

She quieted, then picked up her fork once again, taking a bite, intent on chewing, and swallowing the food, which felt and tasted more like cardboard.

"The only thing you think about is money. You don't care about us," Gregory hissed under his breath. Holding his fork in a tight fist, he tapped it repeatedly against the table.

Alarmed, she glanced at him unsure as to whether he was speaking to her and therefore wanted an answer or if he was talking to himself. Quickly, she averted her eyes to the boys, noisily eating and chewing, unconcerned with the grownups for the moment.

Tuesday decided not to speak, instead to look down at her food and continue to eat, as a thought in her mind raced crazily back and forth; undecided about whether she should leave the table or hold her position.

Forcing a calm demeanor, she watched him from the corner of her eye; and continued to eat. Carefully wiping her mouth, after a time, she excused herself; got up from the table and walked slowly up the stairs to their bedroom. No sooner than she'd closed the door, she heard something hit glass and imagined mashed potatoes spattered on the Cornell Barnes rendition of *The Last Supper* painting he'd sat across from.

Always one to love a fight, the little booger in his mind sprung into action. *"Get that whore! Who does she think she is, jumping up from the table, leaving us sittin' there like fools?*

She's using you, playing you like the jackass fiddle-dee-dee you are. You dumb shit! Are you going to let her get away with that? When are you going to act like a man? Isn't it bad enough the way everybody knows about the motherfuckin' guy at the office? She doesn't even try to be discreet. Now this. Makin' you look like a damn punk in front of your own boys."

Listening, as he bound up the stairs, she visualized the scowl on his face and locked the door.

"Open this door or I'll kick your ass! Tuesday. Open the door! NOW!"

Standing frozen, she listened to him screaming obscenities from the other side of the door.

Gregory began kicking the door.

Tuesday jumped, then, ran to the phone.

Gregory kicked harder until the knob fell off.

Once in, he grabbed the phone from her and seized her by the back of the neck. Using his elbow he pummeled her in the chest knocking her to the floor at the same time. He kicked her in the head and stomach and dragged her by the hair to the toilet, where he stuck her head in and held her face down in the water.

She kicked and lashed out at him.

All the while Gregory spouted one filthy thing after another, calling her every name but her own, making accusations so debase as to embarrass the devil himself.

"This is more like it, dumb ass. This is what she needed. A good ass-whoopin'. Take off your belt. Use it! I bet she'll come around now. I bet you won't hear another goddamn word about him again in this house. Serves the whore right."

She knew he wouldn't pause until she surrendered, so she stopped struggling and became perfectly still, kneeling in front of him.

Holding her breath, the wait seemed to take years.

"Now what's she tryin' to pull just sitting here?"

Holding her by her hair, he began to loosen his belt.

"That's it. Whoop her fuckin' ass.

"Oh. Whoaaa... buddy. Feels like you got somethin' else in mind. Ohhh... Okay."

Something about this excited him.

Jammed up in the small space, Tuesday felt him growing hard against her. As chaotic as it had all begun, it ended just as out of kilter when still holding her, he removed his belt and pulled down his pants.

She fainted from the lack of oxygen.

Later, Tuesday awoke in her own bed, emotionless; unsure about how long she'd been there; not knowing how much longer she would be able to deal with the strain of this craziness. She knew if they kept it up, he would probably kill her.

When she tried to stand, she felt the pain. Remembering how Gregory had started to loosen his pants before she lost consciousness, she understood what he'd done while she was out. The sheets were bloodstained. Holding the sink for support, she examined herself with a mirror then showered and washed her hair. Afterwards, she towel dried and opened the medicine cabinet searching for aspirin. She searched for some ointment to soothe her cuts and bruises, knocking over his aftershave in the process. It filled the small room with a nauseating sweetness. Her entire body ached.

Although it was still early, she dressed in a soft cotton nightgown. Changing the sheets, she made the bed; then stood, wondering what to do next.

Sitting on the edge of the bed, she reached for the phone. Deciding to call the police, she pressed nine, then one; then it became impossible for her to push the number again.

Did she really want her husband to go to jail? The answer was no. She placed the phone back in its cradle and walked to the other side of the room. Standing at the window, she looked to the evening sky searching for answers. But none came. Tears welled up in her eyes, but dried just as soon. She knew there was no sense in crying. At the same time she wondered just what was the answer, if not tears.

Hearing a noise from behind rattled her briefly, but only for a second. She felt numb.

"Mommy."

Turning, she looked up, to see Gregory as he stood in the doorway holding two of her children; one in his arms, like a sack of potatoes, the other on his back. He helped her hold one child in each of her arms and watched while she smothered them with kisses.

"I really need to talk, Tuesday. Let me bathe the kids. It'll give you some time to relax."

Unable to speak, Tuesday offered the children back to him.

"What if I get the them settled and find you so we can talk later?"

Silently, Tuesday agreed, needing all the time she could get to pull herself back together. It wasn't just the situation with Gregory; she also needed time to look over her cases for the following day's work.

Tuesday went downstairs into her home office and turned her concentration to the first case.

A few hours later while still poring over her papers, she was caught off guard when Gregory came into the room. She leaped out of her chair.

He went straight to her and held her in a tight embrace.

"See, that's what I wanted to talk about. I can see how afraid you are of me. That's why we need to talk."

Tuesday recoiled, and her eyes closed into slits. She was suspiciously unsure of his next move. He was right. She was scared to death of him.

"Can you stop working for a while so we can talk?" he asked, head low.

"Yes. Of course," she murmured not looking directly at him. Putting away her papers, she decided to agree with anything he said, at least for the time being. "Should we go into the family room where we can both sit?"

He nodded in agreement.

They went into the next room. She sat uncomfortably. Gregory sat down on the sofa next to her. She was surprised and confused, because he seemed to be his natural old self, the Gregory she'd married.

"Tue, I need you." He reached for her hand. She wanted to pull away, but did not.

"I need help. You probably know that, already. I don't understand what's happening to me. I don't know why I hit you, or why I did what I did after you passed out."

"You know why. It's to get even, because she's using you, fool. Because, asshole, she doesn't give a shit about you. And because… Dummy. She likes it. She's a slut," the voice said.

Ignoring it, he went on.

"I can't seem to stop myself. It's as if something in me is making me say and do things. I mean, like, for one thing, I can't stop feeling like you're a threat, trying to push me around, use me.... I feel like I'm defending myself."

His grip on her hand was tight.

She felt trapped and wanted him to let go.

"Something in me feels, split..." Gregory whispered this last part. Then he dropped to his knees in front of Tuesday, laying his head in her lap.

"Please, Tue, help me."

Tuesday looked at him, uncertain.

"I don't want to lose you."

Tuesday felt perplexed by this. She wanted to help her husband; feeling sympathy for whatever he was going through, but after what he'd just put her through, she felt nauseated by his touch. Still, she didn't move away.

"Greg, I mean GB. I don't understand. Do you think you could be having a nervous breakdown? Is that it?" The question popped out of her mouth before she had considered its ramifications.

"I'm sorry Gre...ah G, ah, I didn't mean to say anything that might upset you. I take back the question." She sat poised; hands ready, one knee braced, heel up, one foot flat on the floor, ready to run if he made the slightest gesture.

"I shouldn't have…"

Gregory cut her off. "Maybe so. I don't know," answering the question in muffled tones. "I just know that I love you. You've got to believe me."

She started to relax.

"The kids and I love you, too, Greg. We have a good thing goin' here for the most part. But we have got to put the violence to an end."

"I know. I promise I'll never lay a hand on you ever again. I swear."

She looked at him as if for conformation. "And then there's the boys to think about. What kind of impression are we making on them? I don't know if they know what's going on, but eventually, they'll catch on. And how do you want them to grow up? You're a good father. They need you. You've been a good husband up 'til now. I need you. But, I don't understand, Gregory. What's going on? Huh? Tell me."

He lifted his head from her lap. There were tears in his eyes. "I don't know. All I know is that I love you. I love the boys. And I don't want to lose you. I want us to be a family. You've got to believe me."

"You're not going to lose me. Don't worry." Tuesday kissed the top of his head, caressing his shoulders. "I made a vow and I intend to keep it."

His eyes darted as the voice inside his head hissed extreme vulgarities.

Tuesday went down on her knees beside him. "I'll help you. Just tell me what to do." She held him close so that he couldn't see the fear in her eyes. But he had already looked away, to hide the uncertainty in his.

Later that night they made more promises to each other. And since it was the first time he had ever hit her, Tuesday forgave him. Making love to Gregory that night was different. The fight had changed everything and neither was willing to talk about it. But he was gentle with her, treating her oh-so tenderly; and for that she was grateful. Gently, he kissed her lips. She closed her eyes and began to cry. They loved the night away in a speechless silence, as if the slightest sound would break the spell of peace and cause the total release of Hades fury.

CHAPTER FIVE

The week began peacefully enough. The children visited with their grandparents down at the shore. Tuesday had no idea how to help her husband, but was thankful to have had a rational conversation with him for the moment. A suggestion occurred to her.

"Greg. Baby, you remember our conversation from last week, where you asked for my help?"

"Yeah?"

"Well, I was wondering... do you think you would benefit from therapy?"

"I can't. I'll lose my job. Besides, I'm okay now."

The voice had quieted itself. No longer was it satisfied with mere words, as it settled in to become more a part of him. It wanted to be a part of the action.

"You sure? I'm trying to give my help the best way I know how, Sweetie. Okay?" She spoke softly.

He stopped what he was doing to look at her. "But, Tue, you know I can't go into therapy. I'll lose my job if they find out. Don't you understand?"

"Hmmm," she looked him directly in the eye, nodding. "There's gotta be something we can do." She didn't push though. At least there was peace between them and some laughter, now and again. Let it go, for now, she thought.

They had just finished dinner, and it was his turn to do the dishes. She was helping to put away the last few pieces when she thought out loud, "Greg, how about we ride down to West River Drive and go for a walk?"

"Sounds good to me." He peered out the window. "It looks like it's going to be a beautiful sunset. I'll go get my keys."

They drove, then, finding the right space parked the car. It was a pleasant July evening. The river barely moved, leaving one to believe it to be more solid than liquid, a natural mirror. The sound of an occasional lap up against the rocky edge made you know it was indeed alive. The water glowed iridescent blue, black, yellow and orange as it reflected the setting sun. Transforming the footpath into a lovers' lane, couples walked hand-in-hand, talking in low, muted voices, where, one would imagine, they whispered words of love, casting spells on one another. Spells, occasionally broken by the squawk of honking geese scattered by children who chased them with bits of day-old bread. It was the kind of balmy night where the slightest gust of wind carried with it the promise of a fresh new beginning.

The two relaxed as they ambled along the pathway.

"Oh, there's Grace," she said pointing to a woman. Tuesday felt sorry for her condition, but at the same time held a sort of kindred feeling toward her.

"Who's Grace?" asked her husband. "And how do you know her?" He had never heard mention of any Grace before now.

The woman Tuesday called 'Grace' was getting nearer. As she did, Greg paid close attention to her appearance. He noticed that she carried a plastic bag, which apparently held way too much clothing, and maybe a pair of shoes; an assumption on his part, since she had none on her feet. Her feet were the filthiest he'd ever seen, with corns, bunions, and jagged yellow toenails turned every which way. She was wearing a tattered wool shirt and pants, in ninety-some-degree weather, with a bride's headpiece in place of a hat. The woman was completely disheveled, from her uncombed, unbrushed head and chapped lips to her dirty hands and feet... a bag-lady. A gush of air blew her stench directly into their faces.

"Uhhh." He waved his hand in front of face. "You smell that? Is that coming from her?"

Tuesday turned to face in the opposite direction. "Don't do that, Greg." She held back her judgment. "Poor woman." Tuesday reached into her pocket and pulled out a dollar.

Turning back, she approached 'Grace', about to hand the crumpled bill to her.

Greg pulled her back, away from the woman. "Don't do that. She didn't ask you for money."

'Grace', as it were, ignored the two. Continuing her quiet stroll through the park, she noted the pair of strangers headed toward her along the path; a pair that seemingly held no danger; therefore no interest, for her whatsoever.

"I know she didn't ask, but you can see she needs it. Why shouldn't I just give it to her? Why'd you stop me?" She turned away from Greg, and held out the dollar to 'Grace' who was now directly upon them. "Here, Grace."

The woman she called Grace looked from Tuesday's hand up to her face, then turned her attention to Gregory, looking him up and down. She scowled.

Tuesday watched something liquid dribble from her mouth and land on the ground separating the three of them. She felt that Greg had been right after all; she'd made a mistake. She started to withdraw when Grace snatched the money out of her hand and rolled her eyes at them.

Frozen by her reaction, they stood like statues.

With an exaggerated twirl of her neck, Grace sniffed, lifted her head high and walked on.

Realizing what fools they'd made of themselves, they began to laugh. Tuesday laughed so hard, the laughter became agonizing.

"You know you were wrong," Gregory laughed. "You know…" He had trouble getting the words out. "You know you started out wrong. What made you think you could hold a rational conversation with her?" He chuckled. "She's obviously crazy… even if you were only trying to help." They ran off to the side, behind a bush and fell to the ground, rolling in laughter.

"But, Tuesday how do you know her name if she doesn't talk?"

The laughing had decreased to an occasional chuckle by this time.

"I gave her the name. Seriously… I see her quite a bit, here in the park, when I bring the boys here to feed the geese. I don't know her name, but I feel something whenever I see her. So, seriously, one day I saw her and I found myself whispering, 'but by the *grace* of God there go I'. It was then I decided to call her Grace. Usually, when I see her she's sitting, so I just slip her some money and leave it right next to her. She always picks it up. I've tried to communicate, but she's in her own world." Tuesday shrugged her shoulders.

Gregory shrugged too.

They got up to continue their walk. Holding hands, they found a secluded area on the riverbank and sat on a huge rock nearby.

Tuesday thought it okay to broach the subject and again made the suggestion to enter therapy.

"Here we go again," his inner counsel began. *"She wants to make you think you're crazy now, like Grace. I told you what she's up to. She's the one who needs a damn psych, the greedy bitch!"*

"Me, therapy? You need the therapy. Anyway, you only married me for my money," he said matter-of-factly.

"I need therapy? What money?" she laughed, truly bewildered.

"Always tryin' to laugh her way out of a situation. I can't stand that shit. Slap that bitch upside her head. You know she got a plan. You are pathetic. It's obvious what she got in mind, you asshole. You seen what she tried to do to your food. I told you what she does when you sleep, fool. So what are you gonna do, just sit around and wait for her to leave your stupid ass and take everything? Or are you going to make the first move and set the slut-bitch straight?"

"What..." she could hardly get it out. "What money?" She giggled.

Gregory took her by the arm and practically dragged her behind a huge rock.

"I know you're married to me for my money, but you're not going to get it. I want you to get the fuck out of my life. Do you hear me?"

Tuesday stood transfixed by his words.

"I know you have a plan, and I know what your plan is, too," he hissed.

Tuesday stood with her mouth open, but no words would come.

Gregory started to pace back and forth rubbing his chin as if he were trying to make a difficult decision. When he turned and started walking toward the car, she followed, albeit gingerly, lest he make more of a scene.

They walked wordlessly back to the car.

Greg opened the car door. Out of the blue he said, "So, I won't be eating your food. And don't come near my bed ever again in life. If you do, I will kick your natural ass. Do you hear me?"

Once inside the car he quietly and painstakingly spelled out the reasons for which he had decided not to allow her to sleep in the same room with him. With the precision of an Army General spelling out a tactical raid on enemy territory, he led her, step-by-step, through an elaborate plan--which he described as her plan--to sabotage his food in tiny increments. He left unnamed, a substance she was supposedly using, causing him to behave in an unbalanced manner. Gregory claimed to have proof from a reliable source that Tuesday was further preparing to indoctrinate him with subliminal messages while he slept, so that she could institutionalize him in order to collect his FAA disability payments, which he claimed were quite substantial. Then, starting the ignition he pulled off.

Alarmed, Tuesday locked her seatbelt. "Gregory, this is scaring me. Do you realize what you're saying?" Not wanting to speak the words, she skirted around the issue. "Gregory. Sweetheart, there is no plan. We've been married for seven years. Believe me. There is no plan," she said firmly. But she could tell she was getting nowhere.

He wasn't listening.

She looked at her husband; his jaw set decisively, as he drove straight home.

Stopping the car, he again reminded Tuesday not to step one foot into their bedroom—now his bedroom—and got out to climb the front steps of their home.

Once inside, he went upstairs and stood pointing into the opened guestroom door.

"This is your room. This is where you sleep from now on."

Tuesday almost laughed but realized from the look on his face, that he meant business and that this was no laughing matter for him. When Tuesday moved closer to see inside the room, she was seized by him, and pushed onto the bed.

"Gregory!" she shouted. "What are you doing?"

He turned and walked out, slamming the door behind him.

She ran after, pulling to open it.

She heard a metal clicking sound as Gregory locked the guestroom door from the outside. She tried turning the doorknob, but it was locked. She tried it again. When it still didn't open, it was at that moment she became totally and thoroughly convinced he was crazy.

She stood for a long moment staring at the doorknob, waiting for it to be unlocked. Exasperated, she looked around the room. The lamp. The table. The bed. The dresser. The rug. Pictures on the wall. Curtains. A bookcase. A ceiling fan. She had picked out everything herself and remembered how she had always thought this was an especially nicely decorated room, but not tonight. Tonight it was a prison. She went to the window, and determined that from this height, the fall would probably cause her to break a leg or something. Leaning against the windowsill, she stared at the door. Why had he locked her in here like this? What was he talking about, what plans?

What was the implication, if any at all? If there was some significance, she certainly couldn't see it. Taking a deep breath, she went to the door and, again, tried to open it. She banged a few times; hoping he would come to his senses and let her out, all to no avail. She was trapped inside, a prisoner. She tried the door a few more times, then, coming to the realization that she was probably in for the duration, she finally laid on the bed. Most of the night, she spent awake staring at shadows on the ceiling, hearing strange noises, until sleep eventually took over.

The next day she got up and tried the knob again.
It opened.
She wondered how long ago he'd unlocked it. And, more importantly, what was his frame of mind? If he had meant to harm her, he could have while she slept, so she concluded. But, what if he really has lost it? What then might he do? She was unsure.

On tiptoe, Tuesday quietly peeked into their bedroom. She remembered his saying to stay out of *his* room. But, she needed to change clothes. She called out. "Gregory," her voice cracking. Then again, louder this time, "Gregory."

No answer. She wasn't sure if he had gone to work. Searching with her eyes, she looked around at the hall closets, and again peeked into the bedroom. Gregory was nowhere to be found.

Emboldened, she dashed into the room, gathered a few items of clothing and showered. From the office downstairs, she grabbed her briefcase and went to work. First, she called her parents to check on the children. Then she called back home.

After a few rings, he answered as though nothing had happened.

"Greg, Hi. This is Tuesday." She hesitated. "Is everything alright?"

"Sure," he laughed. "Why wouldn't it be?"

Tuesday held the phone out and looked at it, totally bewildered.

"Do you remember last night?"

"What about last night?"

"You locked me in the guestroom last night."

"I didn't lock you in no room." He chuckled. "What are you talking about?"

"Okay. Listen. You locked me in the room last night. So, today I made an appointment for us to see someone."

"I told you, I don't need no therapist."

"She's a marriage counselor. I think it'll help."

"She's still a therapist."

"I know, but this way we're both going. So, no one will know you're seeing a therapist."

"I don't know. I gotta think about this."

"Think all you want, Stupid. You ain't got the picture yet? Damn! You are one slow ass. The bitch is probably in cahoots with the damn shrink just to fuckin' put you away, my man. Think about that shit. Think about how it's gonna feel being locked up and that slut laughin' all the way to the fucking bank."

"What's there to think about, Greg? We need help. You asked for my help and this is the best I can do. I think it's a good plan since you can't see anybody on your own. It's completely outside the network; we're paying for it out of pocket, so no one will know. Are you going with me?"

"I can't talk about it right now. I have to go."

He hung up the phone.

Tuesday decided to get help anyway, and go on her own without him.

Sitting in the dimly-lit office, she told of how he'd changed. For one thing, she began confiding in the therapist, Gregory and her brother, Adam, seemed to be growing closer. Adam had been visiting more often, especially since the party. She didn't like it, but what could she say. A few times the two had even disappeared together for hours during a family picnic.

"Maybe he's having an affair," she told the doctor.

"Why would you think he's having an affair, Tuesday?"

"I don't know. He says he's with my brother, who always has lots of women hanging all over him. That's one reason. And another is this thing with his sister. He's been going to see his sister quite a bit."

"What's wrong with that? Why would his visits with his sister make you suspicious?"

"Wait. I understand…you don't know…under normal circumstances, this would be meaningless, but what you don't know is that in the past Greg hardly ever visited his sister." Tuesday went on to explain how (in the seven years they'd been married) she'd never understood this situation; his sister being his only nearby relative. Everyone else lived far away in Rochester, New York. Still, they didn't go to his sister's house. On the other hand, his sister didn't call on them, either. Therefore, she found his new fondness for visiting her very puzzling. She suspected something else was going on. And there was also another new habit: Lately Greg had been leaving for work and not coming straight home. Strangely enough, his sister always seemed to know where he was.

Tuesday felt compelled to tell this woman everything, things she couldn't share with her closest friends.

"I don't know. Sometimes I think maybe he's having an affair with one of his sister's friends... But then I don't. I change my mind, since his sex drive hasn't changed." She looked at her hands. "He's always accusing me, though, and I haven't been with anyone else since the day we met."

She went on to describe how, at times, she wasn't really sure if she actually wanted him to come home. She told the therapist that she didn't know what personality would appear in the doorway: GB the maniac, or Gregory. As a test, Tuesday told her therapist, she would use her banal sense of humor by simply asking, "And who might you be tonight?"

If it were Gregory he'd snicker, answering, "Gregory." Still smiling he'd ask, "What... Why'd you ask that?"

If it was GB he'd demand, "What the fuck do you mean, who am I? You think you're being funny?" She would try her best to placate him but if he were unsatisfied by the answer, he'd grab her by the throat and push her to the floor. He'd interpret any resistance as a threat; which required punishment. She stopped talking.

"What kind of punishment?" the therapist asked.

"I don't want to talk about it," Tuesday shivered. Silently, her thoughts recalling one such scene where he'd slammed her up against the wall as she walked through the door, demanding to know, "Who'd you fuck today, the mailman, the meter reader, or both?"

GB had developed a routine of checking her to see if she'd been with another man. He reached into her panties and stuck his finger inside of her, checking for seminal fluid. She remembered.

If she were moist, it meant she was guilty of having sex with another man. If she weren't, it meant she'd cleaned up before coming home. It didn't matter if he thought she was innocent, because, he said, he hated her either way. And, in any case, it required him to give her a hard slap upside the head. The slap would be followed by his ripping off her panties, then, his knocking her to the floor. The punishment was always the same. There, towering over her he'd tie her hands together tightly with his belt. Vividly, she recalled the scene.

"I love this shit. Man oh man," his now constant companion began one more time. *"Who gives a flying fuck if the broad is fucking somebody else? 'Cause she's cheatin' on dumb-ass Gregory and I already warned his stupid behind. The only thing this bitch is good for is sex. Probably because she had so much experience from whorin' around. The slut. Can we get rid of her soon? Who wants to be married to this slut anyway? Yank those damn wedding rings off of her fingers, too! Yeah, I hear her begging for them, but who cares. If she's got a problem, then let her get the fuck out. Tell her to GET OUT! And make sure she takes those little leeches with her too!"* the little booger said, referring to the children. He hated them, too.

Thank goodness they were not around to witness most of these outbursts, but she knew it was just a matter of time.

"You hear her? I can't believe what she's tryin' to say. I don't believe the nerve of this bitch. After everything, tryin' to make you think you're the one whose crazy. Goin' around talkin' to shrinks. She thinks there's still a chance. She's got some fuckin'

nerve. Tell her to go fuck herself. Never mind. Don't talk to the slut at all. Ignore her ass.

I do enjoy one thing though. I love hearin' the bitch scream when you rip her clothes off and get into that ass. You like it, too, I see. I see the way you come, just like that, sometimes. That's okay though, just force the sloppy-hoe onto her back then lick her until she can't take it. You'll get hard again. At the same time, the whore will be tame enough for both of us to get what we want.

Yow-weee! I could do this all day. Look at how she pretends to put up a fight. I can't believe it. She's even pretending to beg you to stop, but, of course; she coming, too. Look at her!

Now turn her over and get into that tight little butt. I love it! The screamin', the moanin'. This is incredible!"

They met twice a week. Tuesday was able to persuade Gregory to attend also.

The therapist diagnosed Tuesday's reluctance to leave her horrific environment as a condition called Battered Woman's Syndrome.

"Tuesday, I have to tell you honestly, after all of our sessions together, and after meeting with Gregory a few times, I'm doubtful there is anything wrong with him," the therapist concluded.

"But that makes no sense," Tuesday exclaimed, convinced the therapist didn't know what she was talking about.

"Tuesday, I'm sorry, but I believe he simply doesn't want to be married anymore. And quite frankly, I'm more concerned about you.

"Without treatment, it's likely you may continue in this cycle of abuse."

"I understand what you're saying about Battered Woman's Syndrome. But I don't agree with you about

Gregory. It's just not true. And, I'm here for treatment now, aren't I?" She shifted in her seat.

"Yes, Tuesday, but how do you feel about what I've said?"

"I hear what you're saying, but I know how I feel. I love my husband. My children need their father. I can't just up and leave him, just like that. I know what I've seen, too. And if you could see one of his episodes you'd know something is definitely wrong. He's like a Doctor Jekyll and a Mister Hyde. I mean, I really don't think you appreciate what we've been going through."

"But, Tuesday, don't you feel a certain amount of fear and a need to protect yourself and your children?"

"Doctor, not only am I in love with my husband, but I'm committed to Gregory and to our marriage. And, my commitment to him is stronger than love. I believe commitment can withstand hard times when love cannot. And that it can transcend apathy where love will not. Love is a fleeting feeling that comes and goes--while commitment is rock hard. He needs me to be there for him now; and I need him, too."

She stood up to leave.

"Gregory is sick and confused, but he's not a bad person. He's been a wonderful husband and father for years. And I'm not perfect, but he's been there for me, helping me through law school. Helping me raise our four boys. I can't just kick him out. I promised him. I can't jump ship now, leaving him, hanging him out to dry."

She headed to the door.

"Tuesday, I must advise you—I urge you—to leave, to get a safe distance away, for your own protection.

"Listen to me. I'm sure you've heard of the third eye, where it allows us to see things before they happen. Well, there is also something called the silver tongue, or one's inner voice. Like the third eye, it allows us to hear things before they happen. Sometimes, in a situation where we are under great stress, or under the influence of some chemical drug, these things can give us misinformation. But, under normal circumstances the silver tongue and the third eye can be very useful.

"You put it all together, it's called intuition. I want you to use yours around Gregory. Before something bad happens, I want you to listen to your silver tongue and see with your third eye. Use your intuition. Just keep safe."

CHAPTER SIX

Gregory hung up, excited.

"Tue. You won't believe who that was on the phone."

"No? Who was it?"

"Griffin! Griffin calling to say he's gonna be in town for his family reunion, starting tomorrow. Can you believe it? Ol' Griff. I can't wait to see him."

Griffin arrived at their house late in the evening. Tuesday made sandwiches and served iced tea. They sat on the back patio near the pool, making small talk.

"So, what brings you to Philly this time?"

"You know part of my family is from here, Man."

"Oh yeah. Right."

Even though Griffin had been the best man at their wedding, Tuesday didn't know him very well. Basically, all she knew was that he had been in the Air Force stationed in Okinawa with Gregory the year before she met him. And, that they'd studied together for the FAA air traffic controller's exam, and helped each other pass, before their discharge from the Air Force. He was handsome, like most of Gregory's friends. Taller than Greg, he used his hands as he spoke, dribbling and ducking, like a defensive basketball player. All in all, he seemed cool. Like she and

Greg, he was married, but unlike them, he was divorcing his second wife.

"Yeah, wish the reunion would'a been last month. It would'a been perfect timin' for your surprise party, Dude. How'd it go, anyway?"

Gregory exchanged a knowing look with Tuesday, remembering. Then, laughing, "It was the bomb, Yo. You missed a good party." They banged fists.

"Yeah? Wish I could'a been there. But anyway, it's good to see you two, still together. Yo, Dude. A lot of couples don't last nowadays, so it's really good to see somebody make it. You know, Man?"

Gregory leaned back, proud.

Tuesday wondered if he meant it. At times she felt like she was fighting a losing battle, trying to stay married. She thought about the words of the therapist, too. Was Greg only pretending, did he simply want out and this was his way? A coward's way of breaking up. Or did they have problems that they would eventually overcome if they stayed together and worked them out?

After a while, the sounds of the night filled the air. An owl hooted nearby. Crickets chirped. A bat flapped its wings overhead.

Tuesday got up and started clearing the table of glasses and plates.

"Yo, Dawg, wish I had somethin' stronger to offer you. But it's late, and the stores are closed now."

"Wait a minute. I know where we can go for a drink. Tamara Franken's house," Gregory said enthusiastically.

Tuesday looked surprised. "Tamara Franken? How do you know her?"

"Tamara's running a speakeasy." He offered as an explanation.

Turning back to his friend. "Yo, Man. You ever seen a speakeasy?"

"Naw, Dude. I heard of 'em from old gangster movies and stuff, but I didn't know they really existed."

"Well, let's go, G. We can buy a couple of drinks from her. Give her a little play. You stay the night here. Then you can tell your grandchildren how you went to a real, live speakeasy."

From over her shoulder, Tuesday spoke. "You don't want to take Griffin to some speakeasy. Take him to Bluzette's or even Champagne's. Not Tamara's." Straightening, she stood with a handful of plates and utensils.

"But, I still want to know how you know Tamara Franken."

Gregory avoided the question when he said, "But I thought you were gonna go, too. She's your friend."

"Actually, I haven't seen her in years.

"Besides, I don't want to go to West Philly this late at night," Tuesday balked, going into the house. She wasn't ready to go out partying anywhere, much less to Tamara Franken's house.

She came back out holding a dishtowel.

"Come on, Tue. We don't have to stay long. I just thought it would be something to do. Plus, Tamara's about to lose her house. She can use the cash."

"Why is she losing her house? That house is completely paid for. Her parents left it to her when they died. All she pays are the taxes.

"You mean to tell me she can't keep up with that?"

"Aw, Tue, don't be so hard on her. She's had a tough life. She didn't have it like you." Defensibly, he put up his hands. "I know what you're gonna say, but it's true. Come on. Give her a break."

"What do you think I'm going to say? That she has had just as many breaks as me or that on some levels she actually had it better than me. But that she still didn't take advantage of what life had to offer. Is that what you think I'm about to say? Huh?" She punched him on the shoulder, good-naturedly.

"That's exactly what I thought you were gonna to say. You think that all a person has to do is think positive and that everything is gonna be fine. That all their dreams will come true. That with a little hard work and planning a genie will come, poof, out of some bottle somewhere and make everything happen."

"Yo. Hey. Hold on. I thought you two were happily married. What's goin' on here?"

Yo. Man, she thinks you can decide how your life is gonna be and things just happen."

"Griffin. How do you make life work for you?" Tuesday asked.

"I'on't know. I ain't sure what you mean." Griffin dodged the question as best he could.

"Don't you decide what it is you want? Isn't that how you two got to be air traffic controllers? You made a plan, right? Then you worked like hell to make it happen, right?"

"Yeah. I guess you're right," said Griffin, bowing his head, dribbling up court; having been unable to dodge the direct hit.

"Well, that's all I'm talkin' about. It's not a genie in a bottle. But it seems like it when everything works out. People think it's magic. They never think about the planning and hard work that went into it. That's all I'm saying."

"And I'm saying that Tamara is tryin'. Maybe she has a plan, but; it hasn't worked out for her just yet." Gregory smirked.

"The least we can do is buy a couple of drinks from her, right?" Griffin added, smiling weakly.

They made a good case.

"Come on, Tuesday."

"Okay," she gave in. "But I can see her parents now, turning over in their graves."

Tuesday gave up the front seat to Griffin and sat in the back watching the streets of her upscale district, in the East Oak Lane section of Philadelphia, disappear and change from classy, to something less. The large, lush trees that enveloped and surrounded her home (the ones that gave her the safe feeling of being cloaked by nature) suddenly disappeared. Replacing them were scrawny little saplings scattered here and there. She felt naked and vulnerable. Then there was the contradiction at the corner of every street, a bar on one side and a church on the other. Graffiti ran rampant throughout. At this time of night, the profanity and scrawled, misspelled messages on the walls made her shiver and wonder why the parents of these children called 'Dude', 'Mad Dog' and 'My-T-Fine' didn't recognize their children's nicknames. She'd make them wash it off. These were the houses of their neighbors.

She couldn't remember the last time she had been in the old neighborhood, but as Gregory drove closer, the memories of it returned. She and her brother were born and raised in the place they were fast approaching, on the same street as Tamara. A long time ago it had been a working-class area where the whites had moved out as fast as they could to escape the onslaught of middle-class home buyers who were investing their hard-earned dollars in the American dream.   The African-American dreamers who moved in were mostly government workers--City, State and Federal--who had at length, made enough money to afford something with a little yard in a nice, clean neighborhood. By the time Tuesday was ready for junior high school though, the place had changed so much so, her schoolteacher parents decided to move once more, into the suburbs. That's where Tuesday met Millie.

Now, she wondered about this bright idea of Gregory's.

How had he and Tamara become friends, anyway? She thought.

"Greg." She asked from the back seat. "How did you meet Tamara?   And how do you know about her speakeasy?"

"Adam introduced us. And the last time I talked to him, he told me about it."

"Adam? Oh," said Tuesday and sat back.

Gregory found a parking space near the end of the block, and the three of them walked back to Tamara's. Tuesday was back on her old street, the street she had come home to as a newborn baby. She'd felt safe growing up here, but now she wasn't so sure. They continued to the house, a two-story row home, and knocked.

After a short wait, the door opened.

Tamara, a young woman--Adam's age of twenty-seven--beamed at her new guests, showing off a broken tooth. Her brown skin had a chalky whiteness about it. Her hair looked thin and brittle. She seemed frail and old.

She could easily pass for forty, thought Tuesday. Her cheeks were sunken; her lips thin, and cracked. A sagging blouse exposed bony shoulders.

Tamara greeted her warmly. "How you doin'? Gir-ir-rl, it's been a *long* time!" She pulled Tuesday inside the vestibule with a hug, making her feel ashamed about not wanting to come earlier.

"You lookin' good. Girl, you still look the same. Short," she laughed.

"You look the same as you did when we was kids, wid yo' big eyes." Still laughing, she nudged Tuesday on the shoulder good-naturedly, and gave her a slight shove.

With a skinny arm, Tamara showed the three in, inviting them to her makeshift nightclub in the basement. They gave her their drink orders, and Tamara left to go fill them. Gregory and Griffin started to run off at the mouth about old times. Tuesday felt like window dressing.

When Tamara returned with their drinks, Tuesday took hers and asked, "Tamara, would it be okay if I looked around? I see your parent's glass figurine collection is still here. I remember being fascinated by it when we were kids."

"Well, it's still here, Girlfriend. I sho' don't know what else to do wid it."

"Do you mind if I roam around to look at it now?"

Tuesday let Gregory know what she was doing. She left the mock nightclub in the basement, and went up to the quiet living room.

Delighted that the hand-blown glass figures were on the same shelves as she remembered, she touched them, feeling a surge of power. She was a grownup now. Now, she was old enough to touch any one of them. She had a sense of giddiness, made doubly so from the strong drink and from the girlish pleasure that overpowered her. There were rocking horses, ladies with parasols, dogs, cats, elephants and unicorns. They were in all shapes, sizes and colors. There were clowns, dinosaurs, and television sets. There were little family settings, bells that tinkled, cars and more bells of every vibrant color imaginable. They were on shelves in every room, filling every nook and cranny, all over the first floor.

Tamara came into the room.

"There's mo' upstairs, if you wanna see, Tue."

She was right. They filled the walls of every room, including the bathroom. The glass had such a magical appeal, twinkling, like diamonds. Tuesday felt like a little girl again.

Tamara went into one of the bedrooms and motioned to her.

"Come on in and have a seat. I'm just gonna get a little a this."

Somewhat woozy from the drink, Tuesday stumbled backward and sat with her back leaning against the dresser as Tamara lit a match to a hookah and sucked at it. Tamara's cheeks puffed out like a jazz trumpeter; she pounded gently at her thin chest then extended the glass pipe to Tuesday.

"Here, take a hit," Tamara offered, trying to talk and hold her breath at the same time.

"No, thanks." Tuesday smiled politely. She wanted to laugh, too. She'd never seen anyone smoke a hookah before; but she knew what it was, from the Blaxploitation movies of the seventies.

She did laugh when Tamara suddenly flipped the pipe upside down and continued to draw from it.

"Aren't you going to lose your hashish, turning it upside down like that?"

"No, Chile. This ain't no hash," she said in between gasps.

"This here is cocaine. You ain't never seen nobody smoke befo', huh?"

"No," Tuesday admitted.

"How can you smoke cocaine? Isn't it a powder?"

"You ain't never tried this?" Tamara looked puzzled.

"*You sure?*" she smiled mischievously.

"Seen cocaine once and actually tried sniffing it at a party with my brother and some of his musician friends. I didn't really feel anything though. My nose felt a little numb, that was about all."

"This here is different; ain't no powder, this is freebasin'," Tamara said. "See." She held out a small package.

"This how it come, in a ball. I broke off a piece about yea-big, the size of a pencil eraser and stuck it in this here." Pointing to the pipe's bowl.

"That was a while ago. Now, what's left is the whichchamacallit... the residue. See?"

Turning the pipe upside down again and inhaling deeply, Tamara demonstrated how the gummy essence of the freebased cocaine had become trapped onto the screen inside the head of the pipe.

"This the best part," she coughed, pounding gently at her chest.

"Gir-ir-rl, you sho' you don't wanna try none?"

All Tuesday could do was to sit there and stare. She'd heard all of the horror stories about drugs, especially crack and freebased cocaine. And how people had become instantly addicted. She had heard how grown adults had had their lives, families and careers ruined in the flash of an instant...with just one puff of that stuff. She sat, appalled by the idea of Tamara sucking her life away. Watching, she felt helpless, as Tamara finished pulling as much of it into her lungs as she could.

Downstairs, Gregory was distracted by the nagging utterances in his ear. On the one hand, he was glad to be talking here and now with his friend, but on the other hand he wondered what was going on with Tuesday. Where was she? He knew he had said it was okay, but what was taking so long? Why did she feel the sudden urge to roam through this woman's house?

"You know why. What the fuck do you think is goin' on upstairs? She's up there getting high with Tamara. You been lettin' that pussy go to your head. You thought she was Little Miss Perfect, didn't you? Well, now you know, you dumbasshole. I been tellin' you all along. Now you know."

Tamara stood, suddenly. "I need a pack of cigarettes. Come on, let's walk to the store."

Tuesday's eyes widened. Again, she was appalled. "It's two o'clock in the morning you know, don't you, Tamara?"

Tamara chuckled. "You been in those suburbs for too long, Chile. It's still summer. E'erbody's out. It's Saturday night, too. Come on."

Tamara didn't seem to mind as the store clerk passed her cigarettes through a small opening in the bulletproof glass. Tuesday hated it. She was offended by the practice, but understood the need for bulletproof glass in the old neighborhood. Much had changed since the time they lived here. She looked around at the debris as they walked back. Broken glass and empty cans carelessly tossed on the sidewalk sparkled like so many jewels in the night, jewels to those whose lips were quenched by those cans. But she knew that by the light of day that same rubbish would make the area look like a junkyard trash heap.

Her feelings about being back in the old neighborhood were all jumbled up inside. She was tense and afraid as she watched shadows approach them from behind. At the same time, she also felt protected, as if nothing could ever happen to her as long as she stayed in this place. It was very comforting.

Suddenly, she was glad Gregory had convinced her to come. It was the first time she had ever enjoyed a conversation with Tamara. Although learning to smoke cocaine wasn't a marketable skill, she had taught her something new about life. Maybe she was living too sheltered a life. Smiling, she thought, this was a good experience, a wake-up call for her.

As they headed back to the house and approached the street where Tamara lived, they saw Gregory and Griffin walking toward their car parked near the end of the block. She ran ahead, laughing and out of breath by the time she reached them.

Gregory seemed angry. Again. She realized that he had planned to leave her there if she hadn't return just then. She looked into his face, questioning. She had only been gone for fifteen minutes, and, she'd told him where they were going.

Hugging Tamara goodbye, she got into the car and made small talk with their guest during the ride home.

The next day Gregory shared his suspicions with Griffin over a pot of coffee. Tuesday had gone to pick up the boys from their various sleepovers, two of the boys had stayed with a group of friends; two were at her parents. Gregory and Griffin helped themselves and were now sitting on the porch, enjoying a second cup.

"Griff. We been buddies a long time. I feel like we can talk straight up. And I know you been through some lousy shit with Terri, and now with Kim; but, Man, I gotta ask you something." He hesitated.

"Did they ever fuck around on you?"

Griffin ducked. "You know, Dawg, honestly I'on't know 'bout Terri, Man. I was the one who messed up with her. She caught me. But, Kim, yeah, she was screwin' around. Still is. Yo, Man, payback's a bitch, man."

They knocked fists.

"Why you ask me that?"

Thinking it was one thing, but now, to actually speak the words was quite another. He hesitated.

"Cause I think Tue might be fuckin' around," he finally said.

Griffin looked at him opened mouthed, then regained his composure.

"Well, what's she doin' to make you think that?"

Gregory described how she was acting and what she was doing and his feelings about the whole thing.

"I don't think so, Man. Not from what you tellin' me." He thought about it, picturing Tuesday. "Naw, she ain't fuckin' around."

"You don't think so?"

"Naw, Man. I could tell if she was. She ain't doin' nothin'. You got a good wife, Dude. Don't let your imagination start to run away with you."

Gregory wanted to believe him, staring at Griffin for a long moment; he allowed the words to sink in.

"You don't think so?"

"Naw, Man. Naw. "

That night Gregory invited Tuesday to share his bed. "I'm sorry for accusin' you of sleepin' around. I really don't know what's gotten into me these days. I really don't. I just hope you can forgive me. Please."

"I love you, Gregory. I don't know what I'd do without you. I just hope you can finally believe that I'm all yours, Baby," she said snuggling up to him.

"I have never been with another man. Not since the day I met you. And I never will be. I love you."

"I believe you, Tue. I do. And I'm sorry. I'll try to stop trippin'. I don't know why I been actin' like this. But it's gonna stop right now."

"Okay," she said as she laid her head on his chest and closed her eyes.

He pulled her closer to him, locking her in a tight embrace.

"I love you, Tue." He kissed the top of her head.

CHAPTER SEVEN

"Greg, the weather report says it's going to be a scorcher on Saturday, Babe. It's rare that you have a weekend off. S-o-o-o, I thought it would be fun if we did something different for a change. How about us going to Wildwood to the beach?" Tuesday asked.

"No," he said, "I have somethin' to do."

She was disappointed, but if he had something else to do, oh well. What could she do? "Oh. Okay," she replied, "I'll call Millie and see if she can go. It'll be a day for the girls and the boys."

Saturday came, and driving in her Jeep along the back roads of New Jersey, Tuesday felt months of worry melt away from her shoulders. As the fresh country air metamorphosized itself into salt air, the pull of the sea became stronger as she, Millie, and the kids traveled southeast along Route Nine, passing Cape May Courthouse.

Finally there, they played in the sand and in the ocean and walked the boardwalk. Tuesday wanted to confide in Millie and possibly get some advice regarding the problems she and Gregory were having, but decided not to. Right now there was peace. Better not to bring it up. Instead, she enjoyed the day. The two women, along with their children, laughed and talked and ate enough ice cream and hot dogs for their stomachs to explode.

The sun had long gone down by the time she dropped Millie and her son off and parked in her own driveway.

Noticing lights on in the kitchen, they saw Gregory through the window, sitting at the table. There were bills and other papers all about, in front of him. As soon as she opened the door, the children ran inside and straight over to their Daddy.

Something about his behavior caused Tuesday to be on guard. She wasn't sure why, because things had been going along smoothly for the past two weeks, since Griffin's visit. But today Gregory seemed changed. Was GB back again?

"Hello," Tuesday said, as casually as possible.

Gregory hugged the boys and stood up. They ran off to play in their rooms.

Just in as casual a manner as Tuesday, he said, "Here," handing her a business card from the pile.

"Have your lawyer call my lawyer."

She was dumbstruck. A lawyer?

"But... I don't have a lawyer."

Although his words were angry, his demeanor was still business-like.

"Well, you'd better get one. Because I'm filin' for divorce." He returned to his paperwork in a dismissive manner. Sitting back down at the table, his counsel began.

"Betcha that shit got her attention, didn't it? You should kick her fuckin' ass outta this house right now. Thinkin' she can leave here pretending to go to the fuckin' beach with some fuckin' tramp like hoe-ass Millie and think we ain't gonna pick up on that

shit. *Who the fuck she think she's fuckin' with? Hoe-ass bitch, just like her friend. And you know good and goddamn well she wasn't with fuckin' tramp-ass Millie. No way. She was with the motherfucker from work. Just using hop-on-the-first-hard-dick-hoe-ass, Millie, as a cover. I hate that bitch. But I betcha you got her attention now. Look at her."*

Gregory glanced over at his wife out of the corner of his eye.

Tuesday stood fiddling with the card in her hand, then looked at it; 'Herman M. Meanly, Esquire,' it read. She felt defeated, as if she had reached an impasse. For the most part, she was going along with his mood swings; adjusting her mannerisms so as not to instigate and add fuel to his fire. But this time he had her stumped. She didn't know what to do. He seemed serious. She knew that the only way she could stop him was to do what he thought she had planned all along; have him institutionalized. But she didn't want to go that far.

At the same time she didn't want everyone in tarnation to know what was happening in her personal life. She realized from being a part of the profession, certain lawyers were bigger gossips than the *National Enquirer.* It would be almost impossible for everyone to not know every smelly detail of her divorce as soon as she made the first phone call. She decided to get the children settled and come back to this later.

After unpacking their wet swim shorts and getting all four children bathed and off to sleep, Tuesday approached him with her case, deciding to plead the matter against a divorce.

She found him still sitting at the kitchen table. This time he had the family checkbook open, seemingly, in the process of paying bills. He looked up from what he was doing and closed the checkbook.

"Gregory, can we talk?"

"About what?"

"You know I don't want a divorce. Don't you?"

"Yes. So?"

"So, I just want to make sure you know and I want it on the record. I'm not sure when you're hearing me and when you aren't these days," she said in a tentative voice.

Feeling lost, she said, "Greg. You asked me to help you, and I want to help. I love you. But you don't seem to be helping yourself."

"Helping myself?" he mimicked her mannerism. "There's nothin' wrong with me that being away from you won't cure. I want a divorce, and I don't care what you want. I'm taking everything. You've never worked the whole time we were married. You were busy having babies. Everything here is mine. I earned everything. I'm taking everything. So unless you want to lose everything, I suggest you get a lawyer."

She rubbed her hands together nervously. "Greg, we have four small children. Don't do this. They need you. I need you. Please, let's stop this, okay?"

Tears flooded her eyes. She could only make out a blurred outline of him sitting in front of her. A tear ran down one cheek.

"Can't we go back to counseling? I think it helped some, don't you?"

"Here we go with that shit again. You keep tryin' to say I'm crazy. You're the one who's crazy, Bitch." He placed his hands on his thighs, leaning forward in his seat in a menacing fashion. "Now, I told you what I want. I want you out of my life. Now leave me the hell alone." He turned back to the business in front of him prior to the interruption.

Calculating that she had gone as far as she could without risking a brutal beating, Tuesday said nothing. She stood transfixed in one spot for a long moment then moved to leave.

Upon doing so, she changed her mind, deciding to give it one more stab.

"Greg, if you want a divorce, I can't force you to stay married to me. It's just that I'm not sure why we're getting divorced. But if this is what you want, then so be it. I'll live whether we are together or not. But, Gregory, make sure it's really what you want. Okay?" She waited for an answer.

"Are you sure you don't want to stop and think about it?"

"No need. I've already thought it over. It's what I want.

"By the way," he turned to face her, smiling. "I've closed the bank account, so don't write any checks. Don't try to come to my bed, either. You're on your own, Slut," he smirked. Then, letting out a laugh, he went back to what he was doing.

Tuesday, feeling she had lost the battle, went to bed in the guest room, and fell fast asleep, totally exhausted.

A few hours later she was startled awake by GB, bursting into her room. Blasting the ceiling light on, with its four 100-watt light bulbs, he screamed the regular obscenities at her, but this time with a slight twist. This time he held a knife.

"You bitch. I know what you been up to. Sneakin' around behind my back with that motherfucker from work. I want you outta here, right now. Get the fuck out. And take those little fuckin' leeches with you."

Seeing the knife, she sits straight up.

"You can't be serious, Gregory, it's one o'clock in the morning." The clock flashes the time.

"Please." She can't believe her eyes.

"Dead serious," he says.

"Without a doubt. I want you and those four little leeches out of here right now." The expression on his face said it all.

Watching his hand holding the knife, Tuesday stuttered, "M-may I please have enough time t-t-t-to wake the children and pack a bag?" She speaks slowly and carefully as not to antagonize him any further.

"You have five minutes, you street-walking whore."

She dressed in one minute, packed as much as she could, woke the boys and left the premises three minutes later. As fast as she could, she drove around the corner then parked with the car running, stopping to think. Figuring the safest place would be Millie's, across the bridge in Jersey, she dialed from her cell phone.

Confusedly, David, the oldest, spoke for all the boys, "Mommy, why'd you wake us up? Where's Daddy?" from their seatbelts, they rubbed their eyes, staring from one to another.

"Daddy's not here, David. We're going for a ride.

All of you go back to sleep. I'll wake you when we get there, Baby."

"Are we going to the beach again?"

Once Millie answered the phone, she put the car in drive. Then, she responded.

"No, not to the beach. To Aunt Millie's house." Into the mouthpiece, she spoke.

"Millie? It-it's Tuesday. Greg just went berserk. He pulled a knife on me and threw the boys and I out. I don't want to get my parents involved right now. So can we come there?"

Millie, still groggy, asked. "What? Tuesday? Where are you?" Then, "of course come here."

"Thanks, Mil."

"What about you, are you okay? The boys? Is everything okay? Should I call the police?"

"No, don't call the police. We're okay. I just need to come there now."

"Mommy, why are you going to call the police?"

"Mommy is not going to call the police, David. Go to sleep, now, Baby."

"Alright, but is Greg okay? He's not going to hurt himself, is he? What's going on?"

"Greg is okay. He threw me and the kids out. I'll tell you about it when I get there."

She hung up, placing the phone inside her purse. Checking her sons through the rearview mirror, she saw they were asleep again. She drove through the dark streets, onto the highway, until finally reaching her destination.

Millie was astounded by the news, immediately awakened when Tuesday said she was on the way. She was waiting with the light on the front porch and a steaming pot of hot coffee ready when Tuesday pulled up. Millie helped her put the children straight to bed, then poured Tuesday a stiff cup of coffee. Seeing the lines of stress, which ribboned Tuesday's face, Millie asked, "What's going on?"

Tuesday is surprised, yet comforted by Millie's concern… something she had never before seen.

"I knew you two were having problems, but I didn't think things would go this far."

Millie, thinking back to the recent past, recalls how Tuesday had mentioned the counseling and some of what had been happening with her and Gregory, but apparently had left out much of the gory details. And that was okay, because she had been absolutely positive that Tuesday and Gregory would work things out. They were both very sensible people. She never dreamed it would come to this.

"Millie, it's really bad. Gregory has gone off the deep end. I've been trying to keep it a secret from everyone because of his job. I can't explain… exactly. I don't know what happened, but he's been acting weird for a long time."

"What do you mean by weird?"

"I mean crazy."

"Crazy?"

"Yes. Crazy. He's been saying and doing strange things for a while, things like checking my crotch to see if I've been with another man. Choking me, accusing me of having an affair with someone at the office. I could go on and on."

Millie shakes her head. Tears fill her eyes. "Do the words; commitment, honesty, loyalty, or trust, mean anything anymore?" She may have been talking about her own failed marriage, or any number of other relationships she's witnessed nowadays. She patted Tuesday's hand.

"Go on, Tue. What happened?"

"Somehow, I thought we could work it out. I didn't want to lose him, but now…"

"Right. I understand all that, but what in Heaven happened tonight to bring all this on?" Millie interrupts.

"I don't know. I was asleep in the guestroom and..."

"The guest room!" She interrupts again. "Why were you in the guest room?"

"That's where he's makes me sleep. I've been there for the past two months or so." Embarrassed, she averts her eyes.

Millie is starting to get the picture and it isn't pretty. "Okay. So go on. Tonight, you were in the guest room, asleep. What time was that?"

"I went to bed a couple of hours after I dropped you off. Then he woke me up around one and said to get out. I said, 'Are you serious?' He said, 'Dead serious. I want you and those four little leeches out of here. Right now.' I asked how much time I had. If I had enough time to wake the children..."

She started to weep, "...and pack a bag? He gave me five minutes. I got out. Then I came here."

It was only now, hours later, now after actually hearing it in her own words, that Tuesday allowed herself to feel anything, and she began to sob harder, knowing her marriage was over. Here, in this safe place, she wasn't sure if she was crying because of the pain in her heart or if she were mourning the death of her marriage. That's what it was like to her. Death. *Fini.* Never to be again.

Millie put her arm around Tuesday. They stayed like that, until Tuesday's sobs subsided.

"Girl, I wish there was something I could say or do to make this whole terrible episode go away, just disappear. You're my best friend. I love you like a sister, but there is nothing I can do to change this."

Millie continued. "Now I understand how you must have felt when I was going through it. Helpless."

At three o'clock in the morning she looked at Millie with a new kind of appreciation. Quiet now, they sat together, Tuesday's thoughts drifting.

"Come on, Tue, time to get some sleep. Tomorrow is going to be a long day."

CHAPTER EIGHT

Tuesday opened a drawer hoping to find a hairbrush, not finding it she opened another bathroom drawer, then another; until she finally found one.

"Come here, boys. Line up. Brush your teeth." Doing as they were told, she started with the child nearest her and began to brush his head. Already she was feeling tired, and the day had just begun.

Finished with the toiletries, she took the boys downstairs to the kitchen for breakfast.

The unfamiliar surroundings threw all of them out of sync. And it wasn't just the trouble of looking for everything either. It was the tremendous amount of energy it took to get it all done as she struggled each day to get all four children out the door, to day camp. By the time she and the boys arrived back each night, she was worn out. She knew she needed to find a more convenient place to stay. Millie's house was not in her plans when she'd chosen the boys' day camp. Now, rather than being a two minute detour on her route to work, it was a forty-five minute trip out of her way to get there and drop them off, and then another thirty minutes to work.

Taking at least an hour each day, she searched for a place to live, looking in newspapers, talking and going out with realtors. There was also school to consider. It was only August, but in a few short weeks it would be

September and time to go back to school. Where would they go? The best option, the one that would cause the least amount of shifting for the boys, would be to find a place to live in their present school district. It was bad enough they'd been forced out of their home, but to have to switch schools, too? Confused, she thought, no, it's best not to live near Gregory. On the other hand, she needed their father's help with the boys. But was he really going to help, or just make their lives miserable?

She thought about her comfortable home, and sighed. They belonged home. That's where they all belonged. For the first time since that night, she wondered what Gregory was up to.

The days wore on, and as the search continued, Gabriel, the youngest, became ill. Tuesday took him to the pediatrician, who diagnosed the toddler as having strep throat and an ear infection. The pediatrician prescribed medication to get rid of the symptoms and a vaporizer to clear his sinuses; both of which she had at her home in East Oak Lane. Her first inclination was to drive straight there and get the stuff. She stopped to think.

She hadn't had any contact with Gregory and was afraid to let him know where they were staying. But it made no sense to spend extra money on things she already owned. Remembering his work schedule, she settled on a plan to wait until she knew he was at the tower that evening, and then drive home to get the items she needed. In the meantime, she took the sick child to Millie's and made a pot of steaming sassafras tea, sweetened with honey, she served it up.

"Mommy, when are we going back home? I don't want to stay here. I don't feel good."

"Mommy's going to get you some medicine to make you feel better. We're going to stay here and visit with Aunt Millie for just a little bit longer. Okay?"

"Where's Daddy? Why isn't he here visiting with us?"

"Daddy couldn't come. He had to work. You just sip your tea, Baby, so you can feel better. Okay?" She kissed his forehead.

All of the other boys played outside as Gabriel slept. The day seemed to creep by, time slowing with each passing moment, until finally it was time to leave. It wasn't until she got in the car that she thought, what if he's changed the locks. What if he decided not to go to work today? She got out her cell phone and called. Good, she thought, no answer. But what if he just happened to step out of the house, just for the moment? What if they ran into each other, how would he react? Would he be angry? Of course, she thought. But then again, with the mood swings she'd witnessed, who knew. It was no telling.

Nervous adrenaline pumped through her veins on the drive over there. Checking the speedometer, she saw she was up to eighty-five miles an hour, zooming down highway. Slow down, she thought, slow down. She lifted her foot from the accelerator and slowed to normal.

Soon, she was pulling into the driveway. Hesitating, she thought about parking somewhere else, but changed her mind. This is my house too, she thought, boldly, shutting off the ignition. But the boldness evaporated.

Now she was fearful as she got out of the car and tried her key in the lock. It turned. Feeling like a burglar, she crept in through the side door of her home. She checked the immediate area, looking behind the door, then out the window to see if anyone had followed her. Her office looked the same as when she'd left it. Her desk was piled high with the same files she had been working on. Relieved to see them, she took the ones needing immediate attention, placing them under her arm. Confident Gregory had gone to work, she made her way up the back stairway. Near the top, her foot knocked something hard. She stopped to look as three or four cigarette butts and a book of matches flipped in the air and landed in a scattered ashy mess at her feet while an ashtray tumbled down the stairs. What was an ashtray doing there? She wondered. What idiot would smoke on a stairway and then leave the ashtray right there? She stared, trying to envision the scene.

Remembering her mission, and convinced she was alone in the house, she continued up the stairs, concentrating on the list of things she wanted to get while she was there; the vaporizer, the medicine, some first aid items. And get more clothes while you're here, she reminded herself. She was tired of borrowing Millie's things, everything was either too long, too big, or both.

The first items on her list were in the children's bathroom. She opened the medicine cabinet and took out the thermometer, aspirin and Vicks Vaporub, also some Band-Aids; the one's with the cartoon pictures on them, and an antibacterial ointment. Bending down to see inside the cabinet beneath the sink in order to get the vaporizer, she balanced herself by holding onto the counter, her hand touching the surface of the counter. It didn't feel as smooth and clean. It felt dusty, but not regular dust; more like sugar or something granular. She looked, inspecting her fingers to determine what it could be, but couldn't make it out. She took the vaporizer out, stood up, unscrewed its lid, and placed the other things inside. That was when she noticed the layer of white powder all over the countertop.

There was a box of baking soda nearby. Oh yeah, she thought, he probably knocked over the box, she thought turning to leave, or maybe Gregory used the baking soda to brush his teeth and spilled a little. Then she saw a box of matches. She didn't know what to make of their existence here, in the bathroom. Maybe the matches belong to the same idiot who was smoking on the steps. Gathering the items she had come for, she prepared to leave, heading down the stairs and out the door.

Fortunately, she remembered needing to get a few things from her own bathroom as well as some clothes and turned back.

For some odd reason she stopped and peeked into the bedroom before stepping across the threshold. After a few seconds, she remembered his threats, his demanding that she not use their bathroom nor step foot into their bedroom. She stood, vacillating, then, laughed at herself.

What are you afraid of? You think Gregory or GB is lurking about ready to pounce on you, she thought, and laughed at herself again.

The hard part over, she stepped into the room. The small portable TV was in there. She and Gregory didn't watch TV in bed as a rule, but maybe being alone in the house he'd changed his mind regarding this particular policy. There were cigarette butts in the ashtray next to the bed. Had he also started to smoke? No, there was lipstick on them. That bastard, she thought. She couldn't believe that he'd had another woman in their bed, already. She had been gone for fewer than ten days.

She pulled open the nightstand drawer next to the bed. All of her underwear sat neatly in place. She grabbed a few things from there; then, some clothing and jewelry, knowing she needed time to plan her next move. Gregory was not getting away with this. Next, she went to the bathroom. Apparently, the woman had dropped her powdered makeup case and broken it, because there was loose makeup spilled in the little wastebasket on the floor next to the sink. The broken container was there, too. And that same someone felt comfortable enough to store her belongings in the medicine cabinet: She blinked. Another woman's diaphragm in her medicine cabinet? Oh, my Lord, she thought again. This is too much. She felt feverish, starting to get mad. It looks like the therapist was right. And her assumptions had been correct, too. From the beginning she'd thought he was having an affair. It's probably been going on all along. Tuesday decided he was going to pay for everything he'd put her through.

Her attention was diverted. She stared down at the sink.

That was strange. There was more white powder in this bathroom, too. Curious, she touched it. It felt the same as the baking soda she'd seen in the children's bathroom. But why was it everywhere? Tuesday glanced at her watch. She didn't have time to find out, having to get back to the kids. She'd asked the teenager from the house next door to Millie to watch them, saying she was only going to be gone an hour or two. And now she was out of time.

Taking what she needed from the cabinet, and trashing both the foreign makeup and the diaphragm holder, she hurried to leave. On the way out, she noticed more of what she had come to realize was baking soda, on the dresser and the nightstand next to the bed.

Holding the bundle under her arm, she walked downstairs and out the door unable to make heads or tails of the baking soda. She was about to close the door when she remembered to check her messages on the answering machine.

Waiting while the machine reset itself, she expected to hear the voices of a few curious friends, wondering where she'd been. Alas, there were none, no curious friends; there were no messages for her at all. But there were at least fifteen calls from women asking for GB. She was stunned.

"Hey, GB. What's up?" one sexy voice said.

Next, "You know who this is. Don't you, Boo? I'ma be dancin' down at the See-Everything-I-Got Bar this afternoon. Stop by, okay?"

And, "Hey. GB. I'm workin' the Hoochie Choochie Club tonight. Why'on't you come by and pick me up? I got some blow."

Then the words became as unintelligible as an alien language to her, as the room began to spin, and the audio robot repeated one repulsive, nasty utterance after another.

It clicked and it whirled, on and on and on as she could only stare at the thing, doing exactly what it was programmed to do, repeat messages, from strange women, asking for a strange person living in her home, asking him to come and do strange things.

Did all this start less than two weeks ago? When did Gregory come to know so many people in the nightlife? Didn't these women know he was married? With children? Didn't they care? Her head continued to spin. She sat, her lap full with the items she carried.

Finally done, the machine quieted. Only then did she recognize the stench of alcohol and stale smoke as it hung heavy in the air. It was then that she glanced around the room, noticing ashtrays and burnt matchsticks and dirty glasses. Did he have a party?

She went to investigate. On the dining room sat her fluted crystal champagne glasses, some empty, a few with the remains of a bubbly liquid. In the kitchen, more cigarette butts crowded the ashtrays. Three empty magnums of champagne sat in the sink with more in the trash. Still more chilled in the refrigerator.

He was having a blast, at the expense of his own wife and kids, she thought.

She asked herself, *why* had she been so concerned about him and his welfare? It was very obvious that he had been playing games all along. The therapist was right. He wasn't crazy.

An ache in her middle caused her to double over. She held onto the kitchen table, her nails scraping the glass, her face contorted by the pain.

Why did she just get up and go that night? How could she leave her house to him and these people? Why was *she* the homeless one? Why was *she* sleeping with her children on Millie's sofabed when she could be here at home?

She straightened.

Tuesday decided right then and there, Gregory... GB... or whoever he was, had gotten away with hitting her and making a fool of her for the last time. These past few months and all that she had been through with him, had obviously all been a game to him.

"Well, if he wants to play games," she declared, "if that's all we mean to him, then let the games begin." She snatched a glass and threw it across the room, shattering it against the wall.

Tuesday froze when she heard the jangle of keys and the door closing. He's here, she thought. Then she pictured herself pouncing on him, knocking him against the wall, clawing and tearing the skin from his face, removing it with her bare hands and using it to strangle him to death.

Realizing that wasn't an option, she considered the next best thing. Simply put his ass out on the street. She took a deep breath and waited.

GB thought he'd heard something, a crashing sound, just as he got out of the car. Once inside he turned toward the direction of the noise and walked directly to the kitchen, coming face-to-face with Tuesday. He'd seen her car outside.

"What's she doin' here? I thought the stupid bitch was gone for good. What the fuck does she want now? And what the fuck was all that noise? Oh, I see. She broke a goddamn glass, a good fuckin' champagne glass. You be careful. The bitch looks like she lost her motherfuckin' mind."

He approached her cautiously.

"What's up with the glass? Why you throwin' glasses around, breakin' 'em?

Standing a few feet away, she looked him directly in the eye.

"I originally came here to get some things, but now I decided to come back home."

"But you left, remember?" GB taunted her.

Ignoring this, she said, "I decided that you should be the one to move out because Gabriel is sick and needs to be cared for in his own bed.

"Besides, it's only fair, I have the children, and we need a place to live."

"Sure," GB leered, eyeing her slowly from head to toe. He smiled.

"Come on back. I can use some of that tight little pussy of yours. As a matter of fact, how about gettin' started right now?"

Tuesday lost her temper.

"You are a filthy, low-down bastard! I want you out of here today. I have had enough of your *B.S.* and your games. I heard all the phone calls. I saw her stuff upstairs."

She turned to leave.

GB blocked her exit. "Come on. Just a little bit?"

He held her by the arm.

She struggled to break free.

Gregory began to tear away her blouse and bra, exposing her breasts. Suddenly, he gave her a hard backhanded slap.

Dazed by the strength of it, Tuesday felt the room begin to spin.

He knocked her onto the kitchen floor and yanked her shorts off. Without bothering to remove her panties, he pulled the elastic to one side and shoved his entire manhood into her, thrusting powerfully, rhythmically, in and out.

Tuesday lay as quiet tears streamed down her face. Her nipples hardened and rose like ripe, black cherries, as the Judas opening between her legs, greedy for the thick rod it had single-mindedly decided to swallow into its depths, throbbed and squeezed out its own juices.

Afterwards, she dressed quickly, saying, "This is real life, Gregory Washington, and I don't usually play games, but you know what? Today I'm going to play along with you. I'm going to show you that I am the master of the game and that I play for keeps." Humiliated, she snatched her bundle and ran out of the house, driving away as fast as she could. Changing her blouse in the car, she decided that she was going to get his ass.

The next day Tuesday retained a lawyer, finally deciding upon a tall, fiftyish, brown-skinned woman from her own law firm. She had a reputation as a sharp lawyer with sadistic tendencies. Innately lacking any sense of humor whatsoever, a man-eater; Zenobia R. Wright, Esquire was exactly the kind of advocate Tuesday wanted.

Tuesday sat quietly and watched her attorney who, with the receiver to her ear, grimaced. The lawyer shook her head doubtfully, as she finished the conversation and hung up the telephone.

"Tuesday," she said looking at her from above the rim of her bifocals, "It looks as if we are going to have a battle on our hands unless Gregory takes control of his lawyer, and decides to play fair.

"Meanly is gung-ho about getting him a divorce."

Standard protocol was to attempt to get the couple to reconcile their differences. Tuesday knew this. Every decent divorce lawyer made it a practice to initiate his or her initial conference with drivel about a possible reconciliation. Who were they fooling? Tuesday played along with it, anyway. And, after dispatching with the technicalities, Ms. Wright had her secretary call Gregory's lawyer, speaking with Mr. Meanly, himself, to see where he stood. And this was the result of their conversation.

"Ms. Wright, I'm only here to protect my interests and those of my children. I'm telling you that something is wrong with Gregory. I don't think he can take control of anything at this point. He is completely out of control. I don't want a divorce, but; I'm at a loss as to what else I can do to protect myself, and our children. I'm at my wit's end. I've tried everything I could to save my marriage, but I can't do it by myself. My husband insisted on getting a lawyer. And now that same lawyer is pushing things along to satisfy his own personal agenda."

"First of all, call me Zoë. We're colleagues. Second, we need to get you back into your home, Tuesday, because Gregory plans to file for divorce on the grounds that you have abandoned the marriage."

Tuesday's heart started racing. She felt as though she was on a roller coaster ride, going up and down, twisting and turning, moving two hundred miles per hour, looping, turning, twisting, moving faster and faster, upside down, then right side up and starting all over again. Things were moving way too fast for her. She melted like a wet rag in her seat.

"He put us out into the street in the middle of the night, and now, you say he's filing for divorce on the grounds that I abandoned him?" she whispered, incredulous, through her tears. "Why is he doing this to me? To us?"

Men. The image of the word loomed larger than life in her head as she watched Tuesday cry. Zoë handed Tuesday the box of tissues she kept handy on top of her credenza. She had seen this before. She hated these vindictive, stick-it-to-em divorces, and in this case he had nothing to be vengeful about. It was a vile business, but she stayed in it to do what she could to help women in situations just like Tuesday's.

Men. Right now, she hated them right now, including her own husband. "Tuesday, I can't give you his reasons. Suffice it to say that your husband, as well as the rest of mankind will always find an appropriate environment in which to vent the lowest and most, despicable of human acts. But don't you worry. We'll see what we can do about slowing his roll. You don't have to do anything right away. We'll just take our sweet old time. There is no rush whatsoever.

"Although, Tuesday, there is one more thing. There is still the issue of our need to get you back into your house. We both know that because of his unstable frame of mind, you can't go back as long as he is there. Now, I also know there's been a history of abuse. The dilemma we face is that you never actually filed a complaint. Without a complaint, we can't get a protection from abuse order. If we had physical proof of his abuse, Tuesday," she uttered the words as much to herself as to Tuesday, "then we could get a protection from abuse order against Gregory which would get him out of the house, and keep him out."

"He would have lost his job if I had filed charges against him," Tuesday countered.

"I understand what you're saying, and I believe you. The obstacle we need to overcome now is how to get you back into the house so that he can't say that you deserted him."

"But I didn't desert him. He put us out," Tuesday explained.

"I know that. And you know that. But he says you left willingly. He says that you abandoned him and the marriage. He can prove it because you two are no longer cohabiting. According to his lawyer, he says you left of your own free will. You took the kids, walked out, and left him."

Tuesday knew with Gregory's temper she could get physical proof any time she needed to. She knew if she went to see Gregory and disagreed with him in the slightest, he would get mad and hit her. She couldn't be sure how far he might take things, but if she went through with it, the only difference between getting hit this time, and all the other times was that she had a plan--to get him out of the house--and keep him from being able to come near her again. Then she and the children could rest in peace. As much as she would love to sleep in her own bed again, she didn't know if she had the courage to face up to him, knowingly, intentionally, to get hit. She was afraid, uncertain of just how badly he might hurt her. The strategy was deceptive, manipulative and dangerous, but he had started this game, hadn't he? This was something she'd have to think about long and hard, a decision she'd have to weigh.

The attorney went on to explain the law regarding the other details involved with her case. Most of it, she already knew from law school, but some of the nuances in the use of certain laws helped to further her insight. When they were through, Tuesday wrote out a check, thanking Zoë for her time and patience. They said their good-byes, and Tuesday went back to her own office.

Another sleepless night on Millie's sofabed with the restless, kicking boys convinced her. She made up her mind to see Gregory and get it over with. That morning, she called to see if he was home. He was there, so she made plans to meet with him. She put on something nice and drove over alone. Knowing the outcome of her visit, she didn't want to have the children with her, but she wanted to look presentable when the judge signed the protection from abuse order.

Pulling into the driveway, their eyes locked when she looked up to find Gregory standing near the bedroom window. Getting out of the car, she went in through the side door, peeking into the kitchen. No ashtrays, no broken glass, or champagne bottles in sight. She went up the stairs and stood in the doorway, unsure about whether or not to go into the room. Gregory motioned with his head to come in. He stood near the windowseat where she kept the linens, folding one of their brown satin sheets. Probably getting rid of any evidence of his overnight guest, the *bimbo de jour*, she thought, disgusted.

Right to the point, she opened with, "I wanted to know when you were leaving, so I could come back. I told you that I wanted to come back home with the boys," knowing this would set him off.

Instead, he remained calm.

"What are you talking about? You left, remember? And I don't want your sorry ass back here with me. So?"

Gregory continued to fold and smooth out the sheet, cognizant of what his lawyer had told him; that possession was two-thirds of the law. And that he had to remain in possession of the house to make his claim of her abandonment stick.

"Oh. I know how to fix this situation. You bring the boys back. That way they'll be here at home, and you'll pay me child support. I know that's the only reason you're keepin' 'em anyway. So you can get money from me."

His words hurt, but Tuesday was not one to give up easily, and having realized that his putting them out was merely a tactical maneuver on his part, Tuesday let the words bounce off, coolly using his remarks as a segue, leading them straightforward into the discussion she knew would lead to an argument. "I always know what you're thinking, so I've decided to get a court order to put you out."

He flinched. "You gonna put me out?" He laughed nervously. "You gotta be kidding." From the corner of his eye he saw she was empty-handed. His cockiness returned. "Meanly told me you got some woman lawyer you think is gonna save the day. I told you before, I'm taking everything. You get your dumb ass outta here before I kick you out."

Tuesday took it in stride, knowing she was getting closer to her objective. "Gregory, you're not taking everything. I told you that I was tired of playing your games. I also told you that you couldn't win. So, please stop. I don't want to hurt you. I loved you. I still do, really. And when I thought you needed help, I was there for you. But, it seems that wasn't the problem at all. You've been playing some sort of vicious game all along, and now I have to put it to an end. I can't play with you anymore. I have to protect myself and the boys. You have to get out. Now."

Gregory had been staring at her as she spoke. Now, finished with the sheets and, bending, he opened the windowseat, placing one sheet on top of the others. Rearing up, he elbowed her hard in the face.

She bit her tongue, sending blood gushing everywhere.

Following it with his right hand balled into a fist, he punched her in the eye. "I told you to go. Now, I'm gonna have to kick your ass." He grabbed her by the back of the neck and swung at her, missing.

She struggled to break free. Having gotten what she came for, Tuesday beat him to the doorway, so he couldn't block her exit. She ran down the steps and out the door, jumped into her car and driving, went straight to the police station.

Looking into the mirror there, Tuesday saw that she was hurt more than she had realized. Her jaw felt like it might have been broken. Her tongue and her eye started to swell; the eye stinging with each blink. But now she had the evidence she needed to get the protection order. Soon, her children would be able to snuggle with their stuffed toys in their very own clean, soft beds.

The process took hours. Afterwards, Zoë arranged for the papers to be personally served on Gregory, and made a courtesy call to Meanly to let him know that his client had two hours, in which to pack his belongings and move out.

CHAPTER NINE

GB was at his job working as an air traffic controller that afternoon, when his lawyer called to give him the message. Numbly, he hung up the phone, and went back to his station.

"Delta Charlie Eight-seventy-eight, climb and maintain one five thousand," he heard himself say. His mind was not on his work. He blamed Tuesday.

"Two can play at her little game, the silver tongue began. *She probably came over this morning just to get her ass whooped; just so the sneaky little whore could get a fucking protection order, that fucking bitch. If she thought an ass-kicking was bad, she ain't seen nothin' yet. If that bitch thinks she's going to get my house, she got another think coming."*

Shortly thereafter, GB made up an excuse and left..

The long walk from the tower to the car gave him a chance to decide on exactly what he was going to do. The drive home gave GB additional time to think, and in so doing, he made a mental list of his priorities. On the way, he stopped to buy a few things he thought might come in handy. To supplement his already well-equipped tool box, he made the additional purchase of a circular saw, a heavy duty 104-foot electrical extension cord, a pair of wire cutters, a chisel, a crowbar, a box of four-inch spikes and other assorted nails as well as a voltage meter. Now, he was ready to go home. But, as we all know, first things should always come first, and after that kind of shopping he needed a bracer, a little something to keep him going, so he made another stop, this time to purchase a fifth of Jack Daniel's Whiskey.

Pulling into the driveway, he stopped his car, parked, uncorked the bottled and took a long gulp. As he walked into his home, armed to the teeth with his tools of destruction, he spotted his first innocent victim—the seventy-five-year old solid oak antique desk that Millie, the fucking Amazonian she-wolf, who would eat a man alive, had loaned to Tuesday when she started law school years ago. The slut told him that the desk had belonged to Millie's great-grandparents and had been in her family for generations.

"You can kill two birds with one stone," the voice laughed. He had come to understand and trust this tongue as inner sanctum over the last few months and had learned to accept its counsel. Actually, the two seemed no longer to be separate entities. To the contrary, the silver tongue and Gregory had become as one.

"Yeah, that's right. Let me road test this bad-boy right now."

He threw everything on the floor except his new saw, which he put together quickly, connecting it to his new extension cord, which he knew worked perfectly because he'd tested it before leaving the store. He turned the switch. Holding the powerful cutting tool with both hands, he pulled the trigger with his index finger and listened to its roar. With one fell swoop of his blade he sawed the desk in half. Then, with another graceful sweeping motion of his new toy, he cut the once grand old desk into quarters. Let the she-wolf eat this, he thought staring down at the clutter.

He looked up to face Tuesday's reference law library and all her files and books sitting on the built-in shelves.

"May as well, while I'm at it," he said aloud.

He held the blade slightly above his head, then ran it sideways through every book, file and periodical, being careful not to harm the shelf itself. As books fell to the floor, he caught them in midair with the blade of his saw, holding it like a samurai sword, hacking what was left of the material into smaller pieces. When he was through, he towered over the mountain of papers and felt a sense of gratification as he gazed at them, completely destroyed. The blade had worked its way through the covers and pages of each one as smoothly as a hot knife moved through butter. He hoped this would put her out of the running for any kind of serious law career. The trashy bitch deserved it, he thought.

GB examined the shelves for nicks and cuts. Satisfied with the outstanding capabilities of his new tool, he looked around for something else to try it out on. But, first a drink. Again he opened the bottle of Jack Daniel's, walking toward the kitchen to get a glass. But why? he asked himself. I don't need a glass. Nobody's going to drink this but me. And what I don't finish, I'm taking with me. He held the glass bottle in one hand and his new saw in the other. Taking a free finger, he unbuttoned the top button of his shirt; (he always wore his shirts buttoned) then turned the bottle up to his face, taking huge gulps, his Adams apple bobbing up and down. He licked his lips with his tongue and wiped his mouth with the back of his hand. The burning sensation the liquor made in his mouth added to his sense of righteous indignation. He could feel its warmth as it traveled all the way down throughout his body. He took another drink, in smaller, slower mouthfuls. Feeling just the slightest bit tipsy, GB systematically went about his new line of work, still dressed in shirt and pants. He used his brand new circular saw to slice in half anything and everything of importance to Tuesday, or to her children. After dismantling or destroying an object, he'd congratulate himself with a swig of Jack Daniel's and move on to the next item on his mental list.

After a while he decided to get comfortable and come out of his clothes, down to his underwear. Somehow, he still felt methodical and businesslike, as if he were transmitting the most perfect air traffic control instructions over the airways. What he was doing was necessary, of course. He was going to make living in *his house* all but impossible for Tuesday. It was a tangible countermeasure to what she was doing to him, putting him out of his own home. The silver tongue agreed wholeheartedly.

Meanwhile, Tuesday had been waiting at Millie's with an ice pack on her face. She was wearing one of Millie's tee shirts and her own pair of jeans. Calling the tower, she found out that Gregory had left some hours ago. In calling the house, there was no answer. He was gone. Hallelujah. The boys were excited, too. When they'd asked questions about her face, she smiled, but the slight movement hurt her face, so she whispered a lie about how she'd walked into a door.

Home sweet home, Tuesday thought as she drove there. Slowing down, she peeped into the driveway to see if his car was there. An anxious feeling washed over her. Something didn't feel right as she approached the house. The driveway was empty, but she decided to drive past the house anyway. Her intuitive antenna was up.

"Gregory is up to something," she said low, under her breath.

"This is too easy."

"Mommy," Daniel said, "Mommy, you went past our house. Mommy, wasn't that our house, Mommy?"

"Oops," she fibbed.

"I didn't realize that was our house. Mommy has been away for too long," she pretended.

She drove around the block once, shook off the feeling, drove back, turning into the empty driveway, she parked. Once the door was unlocked and opened, all four children scrambled through her legs, almost knocking her down, running past her and up the stairs to their rooms, pleased as she, to be home.

The uneasy feeling returned. Something seemed out of place. Then two things happened at the exact same moment: She noticed the desk was cut in quarters, and a Jason-like circular saw whizzed to life as Gregory popped up out of nowhere heading straight for her with the saw in his hands.

"Stop! Don't," she screamed, holding her hands out in front of her. She was about to turn and run out the door, but was brought back when she heard her children's laughter coming from the floor above them.

GB hesitated too, looking up toward the sound.

Tuesday stood watching him as all her thoughts went into designing a getaway plan for the five of them.

"I'm gonna kill you, Bitch." Slurring, the smell of liquor wafted and curled in the small room. He was obviously drunk. Over on the stairs, she saw a half-empty bottle of Jack Daniel's whiskey, his favorite.

"You think you gonna put me outta *my* home? I paid for this house. You never worked. All you did was lay around on your lazy, dumb ass havin' babies. Then you gonna try and put me outta my house. My house!" He wailed.

"You and those four little brats you made. Little leeches. All of you just wanna suck the blood from me."

Wavering unsteadily, dressed only in his underwear, he and his weapon were a menacing sight.

"Suck me dry. Use me and take everything I got."

He staggered toward her, holding, pointing the blade like a machine gun. To demonstrate its cutting power he slid the blade, unhindered, through the back of a chair separating the two of them, splitting it in two until it finally collapsed, him stepping over the pile.

With a sweeping gesture, using his weapon as an extension of his arm, he cavalierly presented the room and what he'd already destroyed.

"You're next, Bitch."

She ran up the stairs. He followed, sounding like a deranged human bee. The buzzing vibration of the saw followed closely on the heels of her sneakers. Miraculously, he ran out of cord.

In a drunken confusion, GB became immobilized, wondering what happened to his new machine to make it stop working, looking from it, to his wife running up the stairs. There was no sense in going after her if the machine wasn't going to slice her in half, he reasoned, staring upward.

Upstairs, she found the boys playing with their trucks and whispered for them to come. Quietly, they escaped down the back stairway and slipped out of the front door.

Defeated, GB went to the sofa in the family room and sat down, dropping the saw. He looked around the room at the items he'd already destroyed, thinking there was nothing left to do. After a moment, he eyeballed Tuesday's handmade quilt. In some places it looked relatively new, but in other spots the material appeared old and faded. He knew why, too. Because the sow had taken so long to complete the damn thing, seven-fucking years. The dumb ass bitch. How lazy can you get?

He had a thought. So what if it was only the end of August. He was going to make a fire, and the first thing he was going to burn was that damn thing. He got up from the sofa, dragging the quilt behind him to the other side of the room. Reaching the fireplace, he held it, lips pursed, in-between his unsteady legs, snatching the fireplace matches from the mantle while he started the fire. After the quilt, he threw in pictures of Tuesday's parents, her old high school yearbook and a couple of photo albums containing pictures of family vacations and friends. GB picked up enlarged photos of her and him, as well as family photos, smashing the frames and glass in order to tear the image of her out first and then toss each piece in separately. The fire crackled and popped as the melting pieces of paper and glass heated and became brittle. He felt tired, suddenly. Between the alcohol and the excitement, his blood sugar had skyrocketed. Now it was plummeting at a rate of one thousand miles per hour, back down to Earth, like an unmanned missile. He staggered back to the sofa and took another swig, then decided to take a little nap.

Awakening a short time later, he sits in a dazed state. Sniffing the air he noted something burnt and something else faintly sweet. He looked at the tools on the floor, momentarily confused. Looking around the room, he noticed smoldering embers in the hearth and wondered who on Earth had started a fire in August, until he remembered.

GB got up and went to look for Tuesday's minivan in the driveway. It was empty. Was I dreaming? Had Tuesday and the boys been here? I could swear they had been here. Where are they? Nevermind, he thought. They would just be in the way, anyway, stopping me from doin' what I gotta do. He went back into the family room and reached for his bottle, taking a long chug-a-lug, as a small drop of whiskey rolled down one side of his mouth. He wiped it with the back of his hand and went back to work, thinking; he would make the sofa last, just in case he wanted to take another nap.

Going into the formal living room, he made an eneey-meeny-minney-moe motion with his finger, and nominated the hand-carved teakwood coffee table for annihilation He raised the blade. Tuesday picked this gaudy, tasteless, piece of shit, this Chinese piece of crap. He lowered the blade then stopped. Over the years the special furniture cream she used on it had mellowed the rich tones of the heavy reddish-brown wood. The rough edges had been evenly smoothed out, so that when he closed his eyes and used the tips of his fingers to gently explore the faces of the warriors carved into the table and the horses they sat on, they felt almost real. Touching the engraved areas of the table, lovingly letting the tips of his fingers glide in and out of its sinewy grooves, GB allowed the electric saw to hang at his side. Actually, it's a nice piece of furniture, he thought. This may be somethin' I'll want to keep. He moved on to the next phase of his plan.

Seconds turned into minutes. Gathering the needed tools, every door-like thing in the house was made hingeless, including closets and cabinet doors; anywhere a hinge existed, he separated the locking pin, except for the front and the side entrances. Otherwise, he carefully set each door back, lending an appearance of normalcy. Then he went to work on the furniture that was not cut in half by loosening nuts and bolts and screws, leaving the legs and other supports on, making it appear to be intact.

His mood was that of an engineer, enjoying the detached preciseness involved in the progress of his work, he opened the underside of every appliance, revealing its guts, carefully snipping only *one* wire. He knew exactly which wire to disconnect, intent on snipping that very wire, the one which made every blender, toaster, microwave oven, hair dryer, TV, radio, light switch and so on, totally inoperable. GB then went on to loosen every screw in the house, including every nut, every bolt, on every thing he could think of, on every thing in every room. Moving methodically from one area to the next, creating optical illusions throughout.

Hours passed since he'd begun, during which time he blocked out all thoughts not pertaining to the work at hand, making a mental note of everything as he went along, of course. How else would he be able to fix everything, returning the house to its normal condition once he moved back in? And, except for a few minor interruptions, all had gone well.

Luckily, he'd committed his plan to memory, and thought to get his car, which he'd hid in plain sight, only one block away. Returning with the car, he packed it with food and clothing. The process took several trips up the stairs and out to the car, and more time than he'd planned. It would've been totally exhausting if it weren't for the underlying rage fueling his energy.

At last, he gathered his tools, cut the sofa in two, no longer having any use for it, then went to the basement to clip the telephone and electrical lines and shut off the gas and water.

Finally, feeling he'd done all that he could, he left.

CHAPTER TEN

A shaken Tuesday, had taken the boys and run out of the house. She'd jumped into her car and drove two blocks before stopping. Thinking about the state Greg was in, she parked, then she and the children walked from there back to Derrick and Nancy's house a half block from her own. There, she used the phone to call the police, hoping they would stop Greg from destroying the house. Embarrassed, she confided in Nancy, her neighbor, describing how Gregory had come after her with the saw. They waited for the police.

The children enjoyed playing with Derrick and Nancy's cat and dog. Their house was very familiar, and already a second home. But, now it was getting late, they were all tired and ready to go home to sleep in their own beds.

A patrol car stopped in front, and two uniformed officers got out. Tuesday went out to meet them, showing the order of protection.

"We went to the house, Miss, but we can't do anything. We saw what you meant about him destroying the furniture and all, but your husband said nothing was going on."

The second one interjected. "It's his house, Ma'am. And we don't have a search warrant or anything."

"Sorry, but there's nothing more we can do. Your husband said he was packing to leave, if that helps any." The police left.

She and Nancy went to the kitchen. They fed the boys and waited. Hours passed.

"You know, I just realized I can see part of your house from my upstairs window." Nancy called out to Tuesday. "Come here. Look."

Squeezed shoulder-to-shoulder, they peered out. And after a moment, Gregory appeared with an armload of things.

"What is he holding? Can you tell?"

Nancy squinted. "It looks to me like he's carrying clothes."

They watched him load his car and drive off, only to return a short while later, load the car again, leave and do the same thing over and over again.

"He sure has a lot of clothes."

Tuesday nodded in agreement.

When he hadn't returned for more than an hour, they assumed he'd left for good.

Shortly after, the neighbors walked her and the children over to the house.

Stepping through the door, Nancy commented, "I don't remember your house being this quiet, Tuesday."

"It seems just a little too quiet, if you ask me," said Derrick.

"But one thing's for sure, if he were here, we'd have heard him by now. I'll look around since I'm here, but I'm pretty sure he's gone. You saw him leave, right?"

"Where's the light switch?"

Click. Click.

"Oh, damn. The electricity is out. You think he turned off the electricity?"

"After the incident with the saw, I wouldn't put it past him," Nancy bristled with anger.

"Now why would he do that knowing you and the boys were going to be here?" Derrick was incredulous.

Nancy went back to their house to get a flashlight.

"I don't know," Tuesday answered, not wanting to explain.

"Look at this," Derrick said pointing. A sliver of light shined down on the desk, which was split open like an apple, quartered and splayed. Shreds of paper were piled high next to it.

"I know. I saw it earlier. I told Nancy about it."

He felt bad for her. From what he saw, Greg had gone off the deep end.

"You sure you want to stay here, just you and the boys? You can stay the night with us and come here in the morning... when there's more light."

"I'm just tired right now. I don't imagine Greg will be back here tonight, knowing I have a restraining order. And right now, I've got to get these kids to bed," absentmindedly patting her son's head.

"Mommy why is it so dark?"

"Mommy, what happened to the furniture?"

"Mommy, where's Daddy? At work?" The questions from the frightened children were endless.

They turned when they heard Nancy and saw the gleam of the flashlight.

A Silver Tongue   pg. 110

Derrick left to do an abbreviated tour of the house, checking for Gregory, also to see if there were any major problems that jumped right out, while Nancy and Tuesday held the children back, waiting for the all clear. He finished quickly; and after a few minutes, returned to face the two women.

With a knowing glance at his wife, he sighed then said, "Well, it's a mess, Tuesday, but it looks safe enough from what I can see; which isn't much with only a flashlight. Greg isn't here, and I think you're right. He won't be coming back as long as you have that protection order. Just make sure you lock the doors, and you should be fine."

"We're going to leave; but here, you keep the flashlight."

Then he looked at the children. "And you, boys, I want you to mind your mom. Okay?" He smiled.

Using the flashlight to make their way up the stairs, she put the children to bed and decided to see a doctor in the morning about the pain in her eye.

Her whole body ached. The day had been exhausting.

In no time at all she laid across the bed, still fully dressed, trying to think and make plans for the following day. She'd never realized what a great mattress she had until now and fell asleep before putting the first item on her list.

Daylight streamed through the windows.

"Oh man! What a day and a-half," Tuesday said aloud to the empty room. She sat up. The pain hit her like somebody had stuck a needle straight through her left eyeball. With one hand she covered her eye, shielding it from the painful light. Then with the fingertips of her other hand, she gently touched the tender area under the eye and went to the bathroom to get a look. She flicked the light switch.

"Oh, yeah. Right." Recalling last night, she let out a deep sigh. Light streamed in through the little window set high above her head allowing her to examine the skin surrounding the eye, which felt soft and puffy. Standing in the dimly lit bathroom, carefully and slowly she opened the swollen eye to let the light in gradually. Still, there was a sharp pain. It was time to call the doctor.

Standing there in the dimness, she stretched; leaning closer to the mirror. Reflected in the mirror, she saw the novels and other books that used to be on the headboard, now lying in a pile, looking like so much trash in the middle of her bedroom floor. So what, if she had a little picking up to do with the books, and the desk, and a few other things? It wasn't such a big deal. Except for the pain, which was the price of admission, she felt content just to be back home, having slept in her own bed, knowing the boys were sleeping in their own clean, soft beds just down the hall. The lack of electricity seemed a minor inconvenience compared to sleeping on a friend's sofabed with four active boys.

She covered the side of her face with one hand and walked over to the dresser to get a better look at her eye, finding the mirror smashed to pieces. It looked as though Gregory had taken a hammer to it. No sweat, she thought; I can handle this. She opened a drawer to get fresh underwear before taking a shower, but the drawer was empty. She opened another drawer; but it was empty, too. She opened another drawer. Also empty. Another. Empty.

Her dresser drawers were empty, as well. She had no underwear or jeans or sweaters or tops or shorts or anything. What the hell was going on?

She ran to her closet and pulled the door. It opened, falling towards her. Staring at it as the door moved closer to her face, she thought the trouble with her eye had caused her to misinterpret movement. Just in case, she reached up with both hands to catch the door, before it hit her nose.

Her guess was that during one of Gregory's outbursts, he must have kicked the door, or slammed it. Somehow it had come loose. This was dangerous, she thought, making a mental note to have it fixed, and soon. Luckily, she'd reached up just in time.

Straining from the weight, Tuesday pushed it back on an angle and leaned it against the wall. It was hardly worth the effort. The closet held three items; a pair of 10-year-old dresses and a bare shoe rack.

"Oh, no," letting out a disappointed cry, she ran back over to the dresser to check her jewelry box. Raising the top, half-expecting everything to be in its place, untouched, wanting to hear *Laura's Theme* as she had each time she'd lifted the lid over the years, she opened the case. He had taken; no he'd stolen; her jewelry and ripped the ballerina from the music box. It was quiet.

Looking around the room at the opened closet and drawers, she could see that all of her personal belongings were gone.

Thinking of the gold chain with the porcelain flower that he'd bought off of a street vendor, she touched her neck. It too, was gone. Though it was cheap, she still wanted it. They hadn't been married very long when, stopping at a vendor's cart it caught Gregory's eye.

She remembered what he'd said when he put it around her neck.

"Always remember, when you wear this that it is a token of my love for you, Tuesday. My Tue-Tue, that's what I'm going to call you," he said, clasping the chain around her neck.

"The porcelain flower represents the blossoming of my love for you, but it's porcelain so that it can never wither away and die. The chain represents my unbroken circle of love that will surround you forever."

A feeling of panic washed over her, followed by a tingle that made every feathery hair on her face, arms, ears, legs and toes stand on end, as yesterday's nightmare began to replay like a video in her head.

"Gregory!" she cried out, recalling the silhouette of his body carrying armloads of clothing to his car.

"Liar!" she fumed. "You call this love? You hit me! You steal my jewelry! You steal my clothes!" She paced the room.

"No…. I won't get upset. Right now, I've got to concentrate, start fresh, put first things first."

She looked around for the phone. Spotting it on the nightstand, on his side of the bed she picked it up, but there was no dial tone.

"Ah ha," she said flatly. It occurred to her just then that the door was probably no accident. She was starting to get the picture. Tuesday's heart beat with one giant thud. Great, she thought, now a heart attack.

"Mommy," Gregory, Jr., the oldest of the five-year-old twins; the one they called Duce, tugged at her tee shirt. "Mommy, can I have some breakfast?"

David, her oldest child, walked into the room and gave her a hug and kiss. The two were clad in undershirt and shorts. Tuesday looked at them and remembered that this was what it was all about, providing a safe, loving and nurturing environment for them, her children. She kneeled and took both of them into her arms.

Standing, she said, "Okay, Sweetie, but first let Mommy wash her face. You two go wake your brothers."

She went to the bathroom sink where the spigot sputtered and spat and shot out a wad of water, then nothing. Deciding to try the other bathroom, she went there. No water. Nor did the toilet flush.

"That loony tunes, why would he turn off the water?"

Her patience was being challenged.

Shouting, she called. "Come on, guys. Let's go downstairs and eat."

"Mommy," David answered, "come here."

Tuesday froze in her tracks, just as confounded as her son to see his toy trains thrown, willy-nilly, all around his room.

Daniel, rubbing his eyes asked, "Why is the choo-choo train over there, Mommy? And some of it over there?" Pointing to one corner of the room, then the other. It was as if someone had invented a new kind of confetti to be tossed into the air.

Tuesday knelt to examine the train. Touching it triggered a picture of Gregory, wild-eyed and crazy drunk, staggering, brandishing the saw the way a robber brandishes an automatic weapon, maybe falling onto the unfortunate toy that had gotten in his way. Yes, his sudden anger at the toy would have caused him to pick it up and break it in two. She could feel his heat and his anger still within the toy train. She could smell his sweat, too.

Picturing Greg, she saw him taking one by every innocent one, breaking each part of the train in two, hurling the engine against the wall, smashing the caboose on the floor. And then, in a rage against the track, she again pictured him squeezing it with his bare hands, crushing all the toys into bits and pieces.

      She stood, leaning against the wall for support. Taking a deep breath, she held it and counted to ten, then let it out in one big whoosh. She was getting skittish, and hoped this was the last of her husband's handiwork, knowing in her heart that it wasn't. The game was becoming more and more treacherous. She went back, opening one of Daniel's dresser drawers, thankful the drawer had clothing in it and was not empty like hers. While he dressed, Tuesday checked everything in the room. She pulled back the covers, checking in between the sheets. For what, she didn't know. She opened all the drawers. When she came to the closet, she remembered her own closet door and carefully pulled at it. The door did not come apart, but the closet was empty. He'd stripped the closet clean of all his son's clothing, shoes and sneakers.

      She turned to go into one of the other bedrooms, but on second thought decided there was no need to do that right now. There was no telling what she might find. Whatever it was, whatever shape it was in, could wait. She would deal with it later. She decided whatever of Daniel and David's clothing was available would be used to dress all of them. Right now, her job was to get the children fed.

      Shouting, she called. "Come on, guys, let's go downstairs and eat. I'll make you something.

      "*If I can*," she added under her breath. At the top of the stairs she remembered the door and wondered what else GB may have rigged. The stairs? Leading the way she said, to her children, "Let's play a game of follow the leader. I'll be the leader and you all do everything that I do. You step where I step. Okay?" Stopping, she said, "Here, wait a minute, let's hold hands.

"Okay, come on."

They went downstairs step by step. First touching down with one foot to make sure the landing was secure, then bringing the next foot down. The boys giggled at their mother, taking one step at a time until they reached the bottom.

The kitchen was a mess. Now she understood what Derrick meant after making the inspection the night before. "Stand back, boys. Go stand over there," she said pointing toward one of the nearby windows. Where the glass tabletop had been, there was now a big empty hole with a million shattered pieces on the floor beneath.

"I don't want you to get cut or anything. David, hand Mommy the broom."

He did as he was told, then stood huddled next to his brothers.

She moved one of the chairs that surrounded the table and when she did, it fell apart.

All of the boys, except David, jumped, then laughed. "Mommy," Gabriel pointed, "look."

She moved the others slightly; and they broke apart, too. The seats looked like six large Frisbees lying on her kitchen floor. She tried to bring a smile to her face, but the effort was too overwhelming, as she swept the floor.

That done, she reached up to open one of the cereal cabinets. Remembering the closet door, she carefully, gently, tugged at the handle, ready to catch it should it fall when the knob came off in her hand. She watched in amazement, then leaped out of harms way as the door fell crashing to the floor. She looked at the handle in her hand, then to the cabinet. It was empty.

No big deal, they'll eat hot cereal today, she thought, turning the knob to ignite the gas stove. A slight hissing sound emerged from the stove then fizzled out. Undaunted, she pushed the handle on the sink to get water. They would use the microwave to cook. Nothing. Still, no big deal, she would use the water from the pitcher they kept in the refrigerator. Of course, it probably won't be cold because the electricity was off, which also meant the microwave was out, and all of the food was going to spoil, but at least they would have water.

She opened the refrigerator to find it completely cleaned out.

Placing her hands on her hips, she stood straight, looking from one cabinet to the next. Well, they would eat something else, she thought, never one to give up.

The boys stared at her in silence, hunger setting in, as this no longer seemed funny.

Checking for some forgotten can of food, or an edible package of something or another, she carefully opened every cabinet door, which immediately fell from its tenuous position. Searching the pantry, she found all of the racks empty there, too. There was absolutely no food in the house, whatsoever.

Nothing.

Tuesday thought about Old Mother Hubbard and her bare cupboard. So, this was how she felt?

"He's one sick puppy," she mumbled.

"Come on, boys," trying to sound perky, "let's go back upstairs and finish getting dressed. We're going out for breakfast this morning." Bearing in mind what he'd said about closing the bank account, she wondered how far they'd get on the twenty dollars stashed in her wallet.

They dressed and walked to the store. The pair of sunglasses she put on to protect her swollen black eye hurt her face, but she wore them nevertheless. At the 7-11 she bought breakfast burritos and heated them in the store's microwave, calling Millie and her lawyer from the store, to tell them what was happening.

On the walk back, she thought about what she needed to do first. In her judgment the children's rooms needed to be made safe, first and foremost. If she could do that, then she could feel free to handle anything else that needed to be done.

Entering the house, Tuesday went straight to Duce and Gabriel's room, where the situation was about the same as their twin brothers. Instead of trains, these two had racing cars, with a Darlington 500 Speedway electrified track. Like their brother's toys, these cars had also been crushed like ants and ground into the floor, including the remote controls. Gregory, a-k-a GB The Crusher, had obviously been here, too.

After straightening the room somewhat, and feeling sure that the bedrooms were safe enough, she gave them strict instructions and left them playing with any unbroken toys she could find, while she made an inspection of the rest of the house.

Her home office was a shambles. She had seen the oak desk, briefly, the day before, after it had been sliced and diced. But yesterday she had been distracted by Gregory and not quite able to absorb the full effect of his crude surgery. Now, she was actually able to see and feel the nakedness of the bared wood, its insides exposed. Its matching chair could now pass for someone's clever idea of a leather beach chair, where the back legs had been chopped off almost up to the seat. The chair, once regal, once fit enough for the most successful law practice, now resembled a half-witted recliner. How would she ever be able to explain this to Millie?

The file cabinet; previously filled with folders and papers documenting all the hopes and dreams of Tuesday's clients, was now empty, except for a few shreds. There were jagged bits of broken glass and wood on the floor, which she recognized as pieces of the frames that once proclaimed the awards and achievements of its recipients, both Gregory and Tuesday.

Taking inventory of the damage, she came upon the sofa in the family room, cut in half, lying on its arms like two drunken armchairs trying to sleep off a night on the town. Her beautiful tiffany-style table lamps, smashed to smithereens. Sniffing, she smelled the remnants of a dormant fire and saw where Gregory had thrown her finally-completed quilt into the fireplace. She was disappointed (to say the least). It had taken her years to complete. Using the poker she uncovered the ashes of her yearbooks and family photo albums, their wedding pictures and photos of the latest party and all their friends. The one's that frightened her the most were torn photographs of the two of them, not only burned, but her image had had holes poked through it, like stab wounds.

She was seeing it with her own eyes but couldn't believe the amount of destruction Gregory had dealt in their beautiful home. At the beginning she had been confused by his hatred. It was only now that she realized its full extent.

The realization finally hit home that she was not merely a rejected wife with whom Gregory had shared mostly good and productive years; but that somehow Tuesday had become a mortal enemy. This was no longer a game. It was all too, too real. He had declared war.

Suddenly, she was hot and needed fresh air to catch her breath. When she tried to open one of the windows, it stuck. Tuesday went under the sink where she always kept a can of WD-40 handy to take care of sticky situations like this one. Returning to the window, she sprayed the pleasant smelling lubricant.

The smell reminded her of a television commercial where she could see herself holding a can in her hand and smiling into the camera. "Tuesday says, if a dog is a man's best friend, a can of WD-40 is a woman's best friend. Try it, you'll see."

Spraying, she tried raising the window again. Maybe it's locked? What a concept, she thought and jiggled the catch. No.... It isn't locked. It's stuck, somehow. She banged at it around the edges (the area between the window frame and the wall) then tried lifting it again... to no avail. Why couldn't she open this window? She stood puzzled, hands resting on her hips, staring at the window. An uneven fissure in the frame came into view; focusing, she saw it: A rather large nail. She inspected it closer. The window had been nailed shut with a four-inch spike. Could it be maybe this one window had been nailed shut for a particular reason, and that maybe, she just hadn't noticed it before? Wanting to believe this rather than to believe in the alternative possibility; that Gregory would nail all forty-two windows in the house shut, she shook her head. Eventually, curiosity got the best of her, and she checked the rest of the windows in the room anyway. They were all nailed shut the same way.

"Oh my God!" she repeated aloud, as she went throughout the house, checking the windows in the kitchen, her office, the dining room and the living room.
"He's nailed all of them shut."
Shaking and frightened, she wondered if she should have him committed. As if to answer her question; there was a knock at the side door.

"Where's your Jeep?" Millie asked brushing past her.
"I hid it a few blocks away. Thanks for the reminder. I have to go get it, and get to the doctor."
"Oh, that's right. Let me take a look at that eye." They went into the family room where Millie lifted Tuesday's chin; peering into her face. Millie touched the swollen area. Tuesday flinched.
"Lord. I don't know what's gotten into Gregory, but it looks like you need to get to a doctor quick," Millie said, after her examination.

Then, looking around, she asked, "What happened here, Girlfriend?"
It was hard to believe Greg had practically demolished his own home, but; she was seeing it with her own eyes.

"Millie, I feel like I'm in the *Twilight Zone* or something. I mean… you should see this. None of it makes any sense to me. Does it to you?"

"I don't know, Tuesday. As a psychologist, this falls out of the range of predictable behavior. You know? At least if he'd had some history, then maybe you would have seen the warning signs. Maybe you would have been able to help, or at least, do *something*. I really don't know what's going on with him. I would say it was drugs under normal circumstances, but there is no way he could be doing drugs, is there?"

"No, he doesn't do drugs. I don't think he's ever even experimented. I think he would have told me after all these years."

Millie had to agree.

"The thing about all this, Tue… the thing that baffles me the most is that he has no history of drug abuse or mental illness. His job would catch all that, right? So there's no way. He doesn't smoke at all or drink very much, either, does he? This is bizarre, Girl. Totally bizarre."

Tuesday hugged her friend.

"I'm terrified for you. Where do you find the strength to deal with this?" Then, "Do I hear the children upstairs?"

"Yes. They're upstairs playing. There's more damage up there, but they're okay in their rooms."

"Tuesday, show me what you want done first. Then you go to the doctor's office."

They started by changing the locks on the doors.

A little later, Tuesday drove herself to see her doctor. The nurse showed her to a room where she waited, feeling somewhat embarrassed.

The door opened, and with a worried expression, the doctor glanced up from reading her chart. "Hi Tuesday. You come sit over here on the table," she said, absentmindedly smoothing the papered tablet. "What's this about your eye?"

"Dr. Blacksmith," called an assistant, knocking on the examination room door.

"Yes, come in," said the doctor, turning.

A clear-eyed young nurse with dreadlocks, about nineteen years old, peeked in through the opening. "Sorry to disturb you with a patient, Doctor, but I finally have Dr. Weddington on the line."

"Oh, yes. Excuse me, Tuesday; but I have to get this call. It's urgent. I hope you don't mind."

"No. Of course not," said a relieved Tuesday, feeling as though she had received a momentary reprieve.

Jackie Blacksmith left the room, taking the chart with her.

Returning, she asked again about the eye. Tuesday started to lie, then changed her mind, telling the whole ugly truth. Jackie listened sympathetically.

"Don't be ashamed, Tuesday," she started out saying. "There are lots of women out there in your same shoes. I see them all the time. Believe me." Writing out a referral slip for Tuesday to see a specialist, she continued. "My husband and I hit a rough patch there, a while back. We almost broke up ourselves; but we worked it out. It was nothing like your situation, though. Normally, I'd advise any couple to try to work things out, but in this case I don't see it happening. See the specialist. Here's a

Valium prescription if you feel the need for something to help get you through this. Call me next week, just to check in. I want to know how you're making out.

"As a matter of fact, I'm going to stop by to check on you for myself." She hugged her friend goodbye.

Back home, she and Millie called to report the house as vandalized, but the responding officer said she couldn't because vandals were not involved. The perpetrator, he said, was her husband, and it was his house to do with as he pleased.

"But," he added, "I do know something about plumbing, and I can get one of the toilets working. At least you'll have that until you get someone to come out and turn the water on in the rest of the house," he said, rolling up his sleeves.

Before the batteries on her cell phone ran out, she and Millie were able to call the gas company to come and fix the stove and other gas appliances. They called the electric company to turn the lights back on, as well as the water department, and the telephone company. Most couldn't come until Monday.

Over the weekend, all of her friends and family heard about the catastrophe and came by to see what they could do. Each day someone was there, helping her to piece her house and her life back together. They came, carrying food for Tuesday and the children, as well as clothing, underwear, shoes, and, (because Greg had cashed out their bank accounts) a couple of dollars.

The specialist prescribed medication to be dropped in her eye, every six hours for three weeks. It dilated the pupil to the point where she couldn't make out anything, except light and dark. She was thankful it was a weekend, giving her time to get accustomed to everything.   Millie stayed with them.

In the meantime, the family adjusted to the fact that they had no electricity by going to bed when it started to get dark outside.   They adjusted to the lack of entertainment by reading, instead of watching TV.   They adjusted to the silence by singing, instead of listening to the radio.

CHAPTER ELEVEN

She'd received the message about Tuesday Washington not coming into work for a few days, but it was now Monday afternoon and Zoë did not understand why she could not get hold of her. This was the number Tuesday left in her message, saying it was her cell phone, yet still no answer. A little while ago, she'd even had her secretary try Tuesday's friend, Mildred Peeples, but hadn't gotten an answer there either. She examined the sheet of paper in her hand.

Zoë picked up the phone. Studying the number in her file, she dialed, thinking this is the number Tuesday previously shared with her husband, which meant she was back in the house. So, what was that cryptic message all about? It'd made no sense whatsoever. If only people would speak more clearly—be more concise when they left messages, she thought as the phone on the other end started to ring. First of all, you couldn't understand because they mumbled half the time. Then by the time they do get around to leaving their phone number, they say it only once, and then they say it as fast as they can. Added to that; you have no idea what they're really trying to say, because they act like the damn phone call is being bugged by the FBI, for Christ's sake. Had Tuesday said he'd taken everything, or did she say he'd damaged everything, wrecked the house, tore up everything? That couldn't be right. He was given two hours to pack his belongings and leave, and that was being generous. He couldn't have done anything to the house within that time period.

And Meanly, that bastard, what hellhole did her husband drag him out from? She couldn't believe his nerve, trying to avoid answering her questions earlier. At least she was able to ascertain enough information to verify that Gregory Washington, had, in fact, received notification and been served with the court order. He'd vacated the premises that same day, on Friday, three days ago.

She sat at her desk listening as the ringing continued unanswered. What did Tuesday mean? And why hadn't she called back? At first it was annoying, but now the silent treatment was beginning to concern her.

Why wasn't she answering her telephone? Disconcerted, she replaced the receiver in the cradle.

Later, Zoë checked her calendar then pushed the intercom button. "Sheila, do I have anything on my calendar for tonight?"

"No, Mrs. Wright. You're open tonight, but don't forget about the Urban League Achievement Awards dinner for tomorrow night. You're sitting at the Mayor's table."

"Okay, Sheila. Thank you." Then looking at her watch, "Sheila, I'll be leaving in about twenty minutes to go run an errand. I'm going to go home after that. So, I'll see you after court tomorrow," she said packing up her work to take home, files she needed to review before going to court the next day. Zoë was about to leave when she remembered to ask her secretary for Tuesday's address from the files.

Hmmm, a very nice area, Zoë thought, impressed as she pulled up to the East Oak Lane house. Looks okay from here. She didn't see any damage to the house from the outside. She rang the doorbell and waited, looking around at the windows and touching the varnished doorframe. The trees rustled, emitting the fragrant signs of summer fading into an early fall. She pushed the button for a second time, concentrating to hear whether or not it actually rang. Unsure, she pushed it again. That's odd she thought... no sound, no movement, nothing to indicate that anyone had heard her standing out there. After a moment, she raised the heavy knocker, and let it drop three times, hoping Tuesday would appear soon. A young girl, maybe twelve or thirteen, cracked the door open and peeped out.

"Yes?"

"Hello. I'm Zenobia Wright," the attorney reached into her purse and pulled out a gold case containing her business cards and handed one to the teenager. "I'm looking for Tuesday Washington. Is she here?"

The girl turned away without a word; leaving the door gaping open. Zoë heard her call out to Tuesday.

"Mrs. Washington, Zenobia Wright is here to see you. Should I let her in?"

Zoë couldn't hear Tuesday's reply, but the girl came back and opened the door wide. Zoë followed the mute girl from the foyer and into what may have been the family room, or den. Looking for a place to sit, she noticed the sofa was cut in two.

Tuesday walked into the room then. "Hi, Zoë. I'm glad you came by," she presented the room. "I would offer you a seat; but as you can see, there is none. You see this? Look at what he did to our home."

Zoë gasped, "What in the world happened? Are you saying the entire house looks similar to this room?

When did this happen? You mean to tell me your husband did all this in two hours? No way!"

"Yes, he did. Wait. Well, no. Not in two hours, more like five or six. Let me tell you the whole story." They traveled around the house as Tuesday explained the entire situation to a silenced Zoë.

Being in the divorce business, Zoë had heard her share of stories. Although; this was, by far, the most unusual. Tuesday's message became mere background noise, as they walked. She was stunned into a different frame of mind by the number of men dressed in work clothes moving about in almost every room, trying to undo the damage.

Tuesday's words caught her attention. "Can I have him committed or what? What can I do here?

"When I came here on Friday, Greg threatened me with a saw, the same thing he used to do all of this. I called the police to try and stop him, but they said there was nothing they could do. I knew the law, but I was hoping against hope that I was wrong. What do you think?"

Stopping, the two stood where they began the tour. Tuesday waited for an answer.

Zoë, who hadn't said anything the whole time, (which was very unusual for her) only now spoke. She cleared her throat. "They were right. There isn't much anyone can do. You can file a civil suit and possibly win, but you cannot file an insurance claim, nor can you file a vandalism report because your husband was the one to render the destruction. Gregory has a legal right to do whatever he wants in his own home. Therefore, if he wanted to completely ruin or even cut the entire house in half, as one husband did, it is his legal prerogative. He owns it. No, I'm afraid that you will have to pay for all the repairs to this house out of pocket and try to get reimbursed through civil court. Even then there are limits as to the dollar amount. I'm sorry, Tuesday."

Stopping at the front door, she offered Tuesday her hand and said as if to apologize again, "I will never understand how a man could do something like this to another person, much less his own wife and children." Shaking her head, Zoë rubbed her brow as if she were deep in thought and then asked rhetorically, "How does the soul of a man grow from a fertilized seed in his mother's womb, to become a full-grown man and do something like this to his family?" She shook her head again and left.

Days passed, and after the electricity had been turned on, Tuesday found out one, by every frustrating one, that each and every contraption in the house had been rendered useless.

Everything included the microwave oven, the toaster, the blender, the electric can opener, the electric knife, the coffeemaker, the Cuisinart, the dishwasher, all clocks, the ceiling fan, the vent and the refrigerator--and those were just the items in the kitchen. Then there was the vacuum cleaner, the VCR, the washing machine and dryer, the lamps, the TV, each component of the stereo, the window air conditioners, the fans, the chandelier, the radios, the typewriter, the computer and printer. The list went on....

These appliances looked as if they worked normally. They had no physical damage per se, merely downgraded from something functional to, let's say, a useless but decorative toy. Tuesday wondered what could have happened and why they didn't work. After having a few of these items examined, it was discovered that her husband hadn't actually destroyed the appliances totally; he'd only made them inoperable by simply cutting one wire here and snipping another wire there. After awhile; (as a pattern began to develop) her guess was that he had taken every implement in the entire house apart, done no more than one thing, and then put the device back together. It felt as if he'd taken her apart, too, and clipped away at her heart.

Family and friends who came to help were awestruck by Gregory's ingenuity. They openly expressed wonderment at where he came up with the idea for some of the things he did. At the same time, no one could believe he'd do such a thing to his family, "He was such a nice guy," they said. "He went to church," said one. "He didn't hang out," said another. "He didn't use bad language", they all said. But when they saw it with their own eyes, they became believers of his other personality. And so it went.

Her delight at being back home, sleeping in her own bed, had turned out to be a nightmare.

Each morning she awoke to the agony of knowing it would take another misery-filled twenty-four hours before she could get to the next day. Every waking moment was a bad dream she couldn't wake up from. Each hour of each day contained so much heartache for her she wasn't sure if she wanted to live to see another sixty minutes. With each passing hour she felt herself emptied, becoming a hollow shell impersonating someone called Tuesday.

As time wore on, she became more and more the robot carrying out instructions, commands, which came from an unknown source. She was perpetrating a fraud each day, pretending to be fully human, as if to belong among the living; passing, playing make-believe, as if she were fully aware of what was going on each day, deserving of an academy award.

Generously giving of their own time, the repairmen came back after hours to work alongside the people, some who came everyday, to work and help out where they could.

"Can you believe these guys? They came back here on their own time to help me." Tuesday was speaking to Nancy in reference to the men from the different utility companies.

"These men are remarkable. They're checking everything out for me, to get things going again.

"Nancy, he turned off the water and the gas and the electricity in places no one knew existed. But the really hard part is that these men are asking me questions as if I know the answer, 'Why is the water turned off here?' and 'Why is the electricity cut off inside and outside of the house?' "

As they were speaking, the telephone man was going from room to room, frantically searching for Tuesday, obviously frustrated and upset. By the time he finally found her, he blurted out, "Now, look, Miss. I'm trying to understand this. I'm trying to get you hooked up to all of your telephones, but I keeping finding one cut after another.

"Miss, I find one cut in the telephone line; I repair it, but I can't get a dial tone. Then I find another cut and still can't get a dial tone. Finally, I was able to make a connection, but that was it; I've been able to make only one connection, so far. The phone company isn't gonna allow me to keep coming back here everyday like this, you know."

Then sternly, "Did you know that it's against the law to tamper with the phone lines like this? You can get in big trouble."

"No," Tuesday answered, pleading for help with her eyes. "I had nothing to do with it."

"Because," he continued.

"I keep finding one cut in the lines after another and another and another. You have two lines and lots of extensions, so this is going to take time." The telephone man paused, took a deep breath and let it out. He wiped his brow.

"I'll try to keep coming back, and I'm going to keep working on this, Sister, but it won't be cheap. You should prosecute whoever did this."

Tuesday and Nancy watched him disappear down the basement stairs.

"I think he's starting to take this thing personally. He's on a mission."

"This is unbelievable, Tue, just unbelievable. But you know what, neighbor?" Nancy said patting her on the shoulder.

"We're going to fix this house like new. You're going to get your house together and that will be the end of that." She made a hand cleaning motion and clapped.

Just then the gas man who'd been working to supply natural gas back to the dwelling approached them. He'd given up completely.

"You're going to have to call a private contractor, Miss. This is too much. When I finally found a closed valve and opened it, I expected the stove to work; but it didn't. Then I found another, only to run into the same thing."

Exasperated, he threw his hands in the air.

"I'm sorry, but I can't fix this." He was about to leave when the off-duty telephone repairman offered to help.

"I know what you mean, Bro. I ran into the same problem, but we gotta help this woman. She black. She here with these young bloods by herself; no gas, no phone, no water, no nothin'. We gotta help. Come on. Let's see." He placed an arm around the man's shoulder.

Tuesday went with the two of them to look at the problem.

Nancy shook her head as she surveyed the area. "Oh Lord," she said to herself, "couldn't even go to the damn bathroom." Just the thought of it was disgusting, making her crinkle her nose. What was Gregory thinking, taking apart all the sinks, all the showers, bathtubs and then jerry-rigging them so the water wouldn't run, so the toilets wouldn't flush?

She watched as Tuesday and the others moved about busily and thought, maybe Derrick can get some of his buddies to come over and help out. I know *somebody* can do *something*.

The awesome responsibility of refurbishing the house, taking care of the kids and missing time from work on top of having no money, had taken its toll. Once again Tuesday pulled open the drawer where the pistol laid idle. She stared at it for a while, this time picking it up. She hadn't realized how heavy and cold it was before now.

In thinking about the pain of having a bullet smash into her chest, she wondered if it could be any worse than the pain she'd already suffered and still suffered, even now. Deciding that it couldn't be worse, she pointed the gun at her heart and cocked the trigger. The children at day camp, she thought about who would pick them up. A tear came to her eye, and... The phone rang. Tuesday stared at it. After several rings, she reluctantly picked it up with one hand while continuing to hold the gun with the other.

"Hey-ey, Tuesday. Something just said to me, 'call Tuesday,' so I called to see how you were making out. I know it must be terrible over there for you and the kids. Are you okay?" Millie asked; unaware that she was in the process of saving her best friend's life.

"Millie," she whispered hoarsely, choking back the tears. "It's worse than you know. I don't think I'm going to make it through this."

Millie was a trained psychologist and a divorced parent. The two had been friends since they were twelve years old. She understood the overwhelming feeling of loss Tuesday was experiencing. And, she knew better than anyone, how much Tuesday loved Greg. Millie knew what to say.

"You'll make it, Girlfriend. Just hang in there. None of us really understands what happened, it's been so bizarre. But it hasn't been in vain. Honey, you know in your heart that Gregory was a good man who loved his family. Something just snapped. I believe, deep down, he still loves you and the kids very much. I know, and you know he would never do this if he were in his right mind. You hang in there, Tuesday. You'll get through this. And you know why? Because you have to. Who else will take care of your children and raise them the way you want? Certainly not him. So you hang in. Okay?"

She knew Millie was right. She nodded and made a small sound into the phone.

"I've got to go. I'll call before I come over tomorrow. Love ya. Ciao."

Tuesday realized she couldn't leave her sons alone in this world to grow up without her.

"Thank you, God," she said, replacing the phone in its cradle.

Millie was right; she couldn't leave them to be raised by a crazy madman father; who might very well destroy their lives. She had to live… for them. She looked at the gun in her hand. Releasing the trigger, she emptied it of bullets and placed it high up and away, vowing to dispose of it soon.

True to her word, Millie arrived the next day. They chatted for a while, then, she patted her friend's hand and sighed. She had been there for more than an hour and now moved to leave, putting on her jacket.

"I've witnessed most of the ups and downs of your life, the same as you have with me. But this is a doozie. I wish I had an answer for you." Millie smiled bravely at her friend.

"I know how much you still love Greg, even after all of this. But I also know that you're a survivor, Tuesday, and I'm sure you'll be able to pull through this one, in spite of his best efforts."

Tuesday was so grateful for Millie's friendship, she found it difficult to express. "I don't know what to say except thanks for coming by, Mil. And thanks for the pep talk. I needed it. You just don't know."

"Okay, Girlfriend. It's late, so I'm going to go. I've got to get home to my own chile," she kidded. "Just wanted to bring some things by for you. Let me go get them out of the car."

She returned with an armload of clothing for Tuesday and the boys and a brown paper bag, full of old high heels and children's sneakers.

"You'll need heels to wear when you go back to work next week. Oh yeah, I picked this up for you," pulling out a department store bag full of new panties.

"Thank you so much, Mil. I wish I could say, 'That's all right, I don't really need these, but I do. I need every last one of these things, and I appreciate it from the bottom of my heart.'" Clutching the unopened package containing the panties, Tuesday walked her friend to the door and said goodbye.

Millie turned back.

"By the way, I know some people say that being a single parent is easy, but I'm here to say that ain't true--at least, being a *good* single parent isn't. It's hard work. For one thing, there are never enough hours in the day to get everything done. After stopping at the cleaners, and the supermarket, picking up the children, and then making dinner, you still need to play with them and talk with them. Then it's time to give them their baths, read to them and put them to bed. And that, my dear, is not including parent-teacher meetings and extracurricular activities and all the other stuff that happens."

Laughing, Millie hugged her friend.

"Po' chile. But, like I said, you'll make it. You'll raise your kids beautifully," she said, pronouncing each syllable.

"Everything will be just fine. See you later, Kiddo."

Tuesday opened the door as she turned to leave.

They were both surprised to find Adam standing at the door.

"Millie, hi. Hi, Sis."

Although he'd been there helping out with the others, his appearance had been sporadic and unpredictable, like now. "Adam. Oh my God! You scared us. Didn't he scare you, Mil?"

"Yes, I'm shocked to see him here."

"Don't be so surprised. You never know about me. Right, Sis? You gonna let me in?" he asked.

"Hi, Adam. I'm sorry for making you stand there. It's just that I'm surprised. That's all." She gave him a peck on the cheek. "Come on in."

"Okay, Tue. I'll see you later," Millie gave her a quizzical backward glance.

"Bye, Mil," she answered. Then turning to Adam, "Would you like something to drink?"

He followed her into the kitchen, where she opened the refrigerator and got out two bottles of iced tea, handing one to him.

"Thanks," he said cracking open the bottle.

"Thank you for coming to help out. I really appreciate it, Little Brother. I want you to know that. Okay?

"So… what brings you here to visit?"

Now, they were headed out to the back patio. "Let's sit out here. It's a nice night, not too cold, and the kids are in bed already. They have school tomorrow." She sat down, smiling across from him.

"Is this new?" questioned Adam, referring to the padded wrought-iron armchairs and table.

"No. I guess Greg forgot about the furniture out here," she said, smiling wryly. Tuesday crossed her legs; taking a sip of her drink, she lifted the bottle to her lips.

Adam felt a pang of guilt as he watched her. Reaching into his pocket, his hand came out holding a wad of money.

"Here…this is for you and the kids. It's the least I can do."

"Thank you, Adam, I can use the money of course, but I can't take all that."

"Yes, you can. Here." He shoved it into her hands and folded her fingers around it.

"Well, thank you Adam; but I'm very surprised at this. What's going on? What is this about? Hold that thought, though. Because if you really want me to have this money, I'm going to keep it and I'm going to put it away in the house right now." Leaving the patio, she held the bundle of bills, going into the house.

Adam sat outside alone, glad he'd given her the money; but still mad at himself and Gregory, he stared up at the stars. He was angry about being so stupid, a stupid traitor to my own sister, he was thinking. He hadn't been able to shake the feeling, and lately he hadn't been able to sleep nights either, because of his guilt. He felt personally responsible for ruining her marriage, and maybe even ruining all their lives. He'd finally hit bottom and planned to check into a rehab as soon as he left here tonight.

No longer could he stand passively by and watch as his sister's life fell apart. She deserved to know the truth so that she could stop blaming herself. He didn't want Tuesday to go on feeling guilty about abandoning Greg thinking he'd had a mental breakdown or something.

Lingering there for her return, Adam wanted everything out in the open, planning to tell her everything, needing her forgiveness.

Tuesday returned. "Boy, are you intense. What's up with you tonight?" She asked, smiling.

Waiting until she sat, he looked intently at his sister, gripping tightly onto the iron arms of his chair.

"Tuesday, I came here to say I'm sorry, I'm changing my ways starting now, and I wanted you to know. I can see what you're going through...what you and the boys have been going through...and I need to apologize for the part I contributed in making this happen."

Looking her in the eye, Adam continued, "I apologize, Tuesday. I'm sorry. I never meant for this to happen. I didn't know he was letting that shit get to him like this. I didn't know."

The smile disappeared from Tuesday's face. "Wait a minute. What stuff, Adam? What are you talking about?"

"When you told me about seeing all that bakin' soda all over the place, and matches everywhere, I wanted to tell you then, but I was afraid to. I just wasn't thinking. I let that shit get the best of me, too," his lips moved absentmindedly, as if he were talking to the squirrels in the tree.

"What does baking soda have to do with anything?"

"You need bakin' soda to freebase, Tuesday, and you need a lot of matches to light the pipe cause it keeps going out. You saw Tamara, you know what she was into, right?

"And then some people...I'm not saying Greg, necessarily, but some people use the matches to cook the shit in a spoon, like heroin, and then shoot it. When I saw that...." Shaking his head, he turned and looked away.

"I knew it was time to stop hangin'. I could see where it was leading. I told myself it's time to hang it up; so I did. Now it's time for me to get my act together; you know what I mean? I thought it was none of my business, you know, whatever he was doing had nothing to do with me anymore, but now that I see everything that's happened, I knew I had to tell you."

Dry and stiff as a barren desert; his usually laughing, dancing mouth was now grimly fixed in a tight, thin line across his face. Adam spoke with the composure of an un-indictable witness for the prosecution, as he continued with his ugly story about how he and Greg had been hanging out together since the beginning of the year.

He turned back to face her, tears welling in his eyes. "We'd make a run to his sister's house to get high a couple of times a week, freebasin' normally," Adam said loosening his death-grip from the chair.

"He'd drive about a hundred miles an hour to get there. It was scary, the way he drove."

Tuesday sat, open-mouthed, mesmerized by what she was hearing.

"No," she said aloud. This couldn't be happening, she thought. But it was.

As if to confirm her thoughts, Adam nodded, then wiped his eyes with the tips of his fingers and continued. "I was afraid he was going to kill us before we got there. He drove like some kind of maniac, trying to get there before it was all gone, I guess."

Tuesday stood. "No.... I don't believe you," she said waving her hands. "I don't know what you're talking about, Adam, and I don't believe you. And I don't know why you're coming here telling me something like this. Let me go get that money, and I want you out of my house!" Heading to the house she said over her shoulder. "You're a liar. All of it's just an outright drug-induced lie."

"Tuesday!" he shouted, "believe me. I know this must sound crazy; my coming out of nowhere like this.

But believe me, I'm your brother. I wouldn't lie about a thing like this. Come back, please. I'm trying to stop the lying. I'm trying to get the truth out in the open."

She felt pity, as she stood there holding the screen door open; looking at her brother, seeped in desperation, looking to blame anyone for his troubles. Now he was blaming Greg. Her anger started to subside.

"Adam, why are you doing this?"

"I told you. Because I feel responsible and because I want you to know the truth so you can stop blaming yourself. Come on now; sit down. I don't want your neighbors hearing this. Come on, Tue-Tue, sit down," he urged.

She sat.

"I know it's hard hearing this, especially coming from me, but it's all true. Sometimes we'd meet at Tamara's…"

"Tamara's?"

"Tamara Franken's. Yeah."

"What were the two of you doing there?"

"We used to get high there too, party all night sometimes," Adam confessed. "Greg would leave home like he was going to do a night shift at the Tower. He thought it was funny because you'd be sound asleep, thinking he was going to work. I knew you didn't know what was going on, and I felt kind of bad about it, but what could I do?" He shrugged his shoulders. "I didn't know what I was doing."

Tuesday and her brother hadn't been close for a long time. And, over the years, they'd had their share of arguments, but this was unimaginable. In her wildest dreams, she could never have envisioned Adam keeping a secret like this; much less that he would actually sneak around with her husband. The heart-stopping confession made her feel woozy. She didn't know if she was coming, or going. She loved her brother, but suddenly a paradigm shift had occurred, changing everything on the one hand. On the other, they were still blood, and he would always be her only brother, so nothing was changed. Her thoughts were jumbled in her mind like ancient Egyptian hieroglyphics she could in no way comprehend. She didn't know what to say.

Looking down at her hands, Tuesday shuddered when the thought occurred, knowing she had to ask the question. Their father's voice boomed instantly in her head, "don't ask the question if you can't stand the answer."

"Okay," she whispered leaning forward in her chair, "I heard everything you've said, and I believe you, but I've got to ask one question that comes to my mind." At this point she was not quite sure about her ability to withstand the response--should it turn out to be the worst possible answer--she hesitated. "I need to know... I have to ask you, Adam... how close have you two really become? What else has he been doing that I should know about?"

He hadn't expected the question. Adam felt the words smack him right between the eyes. Instinctively, knowing what she meant, haltingly, he took the defensive, "Tuesday, what are you..." But he couldn't stand the pressure of the guilt he carried. Right then and there Adam decided he had to tell his sister everything, including the one time he and Gregory had shared a woman, one of Tamara's friends. Between the five martinis, the pipe, and the blow, Adam forgot Greg was his brother-in-law when he saw the woman giving him a blow job. After that, one thing led to another and the three of them got it on, naked, beneath the rows of glass figurines in a back room of Tamara's house.

Tuesday held her hands to her face and let out a low wailing moan there in her backyard. Her fingers began to get wet as tears ran down in-between them. "Adam, this whole thing is so fucked up. I mean, how could you do that?" Her voice was muffled.

"Tuesday, I'm sorry," he cried. "It was a mistake on both our parts. It only happened that one time. It never happened again, and it never will." He went to her, kneeling. Adam's face was drenched. Eventually, he broke down completely into a fit of incoherent blubbering sobs. "I love you. I never meant to hurt you." Touching his sister by the hair, he looked to her pleading, "Tuesday, please forgive me. I'm begging you. I never, in my life, ever wanted to hurt you like this. Never. Please."

Hot tears of molten lava burned their way down the sides of her face, gathering strength in numbers until they welled into a boiling hot pool of tears in the palms of her hands pressed against her cheeks, they overflowed onto to the ground. My own brother, she thought. Grief and anguish transformed itself into grinding, screeching steel, tearing into her brain, biting through her skull, as metallic bits and pieces made their way down, cutting into her mouth leaving a bloody taste of metal. Her entire body felt squeezed between two giant steel beams grating against one another, flattening her until she disappeared into the metal itself.

She sat. For more than an hour she sat, listening to her beloved brother cry at her feet.

"It's okay," she murmured softly, "I love you. We'll work this out."

CHAPTER TWELVE

Alone in her office she sat thinking, trying to take it all in, trying to make sense of the whole thing. So deep in thought in fact, she didn't hear the other lawyers farther down the hall greeting clients, nor did she hear her colleagues walking by outside her door. As a result, she was startled when suddenly there was a knock, and her door opened.

Zoë appeared, fashionably dressed as usual, with information about Greg, as well as an odd request from him. She pushed one of Tuesday's chairs close and sat, leaning one elbow on the desk. Both she and Tuesday were puzzled by the request.

"What 'things' could he be talking about?" Tuesday asked scratching her head. He took all his things," then laughing added, "and my things too."

Zoë, uncomfortable at first, resigned herself to Tuesday's sardonic sense of humor and smiled.

"If you're like my husband and I, you two have separate closets. Maybe he overlooked something important in his. According to Meanly, he wants to come by tomorrow. Guess he forgot a couple of items," she shrugged.

Tuesday looked at her in surprise. "You know, I just assumed he took everything he owned. I've been so busy, I never even looked in his closet."

"Why don't you check when you get home tonight?" her lawyer said, getting up from her seat and walking back toward the door. "Look, why don't I call and tell Meanly that you'll send whatever few items Greg left behind?"

"No, that's alright, Zoë. Whatever it is, I don't have time to pack his stuff. That's for certain. I have too much going on right now. And, I don't want to put out another dime on his behalf. He'll have to come and pick it up himself."

Stopping before she exited Tuesday's office, Zoë frowned. "While I don't think he'll pull anything stupid, just in case, why don't you have your brother or someone there with you when Greg arrives. Okay, Dear? I'll talk to you later."

Alone again, she was resolute on making headway to get through the pile in front of her. Forgetting about the divorce and Gregory and anything else not pertaining to the work at hand, she got through the day, untroubled. Tuesday picked her children up from the sitter, made dinner, and played catch outside in the yard with the boys.

Later, after the boys were asleep, she went to Gregory's walk-in closet and opened the door.

It was as if he had never left. All of his clothing hung neatly inside. Shoes, lined up on his shoe rack, ready and waiting his return. Ties were strung like decorative streamers waiting for the party to begin.

"I can't believe this." She covered her mouth; with the door wide open she walked in a daze over to the bed to sit down, staring at what seemed to be all of Greg's belongings.

Dialing the phone, she called her friend.

"Millie, this is too strange. I just opened Greg's closet to find all his clothes still here."

The phone signaled a beep. "Hold on, let me see who's on the other line."

She came back.

"Mil? It's Tamara. Remember, I told you about going to her house? She's on the other line."

"What's she doing callin' you after everything? What does she want?"

"I don't know. I don't know how she got my number, either. But, let me go. I'm goin' to talk to her, and see what she has to say. Okay? I'll talk to you later."

"Okay. Bye."

"I'll call you back. Bye."

She clicked over.

The call from Tamara Franken came as a surprise because they had never really been friends and because Tuesday didn't remember giving her the phone number. Now Tamara was on the other end. Out of curiosity she paid attention. Tamara said she was calling to give her condolences over Tuesday and Greg's breakup.

"You 'member when I took you upstairs and got a couple'a hits off the pipe? I 'membered cause you the first person I met said, no thanks and then you laughed 'n axd what I was smokin'."

"Yes. I remember," Tuesday admitted, feeling betrayed by everyone she trusted, feeling unnerved by the thought of what could be next, feeling pushed to the edge.

Tamara explained that GB and Adam had come to her house to freebase coke on several occasions, and after a while, GB had started to come on his own.

Tuesday didn't know what to say, so instead, she listened.

"He musta been thinkin' I was treatin' you to a freebie instead a him when we was upstairs. That's why he was mad when we come back from the sto'. It was right then, I guessed GB musta been hooked. I was lookin' at him. He was so mad that night. Then I was lookin' at you, thinkin' you don't even know cause you ain't never tried it, so you didn't know what was goin' on. I didn't know what to do. He musta come to my house hopin' for a hit that night."

There was silence on the line.

A lot of things became clear to Tuesday just then. Tamara's story helped make sense of everything, because nothing else had that night. She thought back to some other situations, which had made no sense either, combined with what Adam had told her, she decided to believe Tamara. Besides, what motive would she have for calling her with such a story? Focusing, she realized Tamara was talking again.

"I feel sorry for you, Tuesday, cause'a everything. I thought you woulda guessed by now. But I thought you oughta know what's happenin' in your own house. So, when I heard about the breakup n' all the wild stuff he done did. Well…

"I didn't wanna say nothin' back then, but I knew what his problem was. That's why he was mad and about to leave you stranded that night, 'member?"

Her tone changing, Tamara hesitated, then, asked timidly, "Tuesday?

"Can you help me? You the onliest person I know don't git high and I wanna git this monkey offah my back."

"Yes, Tamara, I'll help you, if I can. First let me make some calls and get back to you. Okay? What's your number?" Her fingers scribbled down the number.

At first she felt a sense of betrayal. Then slowly, it was replaced by an anger, which oozed its way throughout her body; starting to build as she returned the phone back in its receiver. Finally, the anger set in.

Drugs, she thought. He was smoking crack, and everybody knew except her. She pulled at her hair, stifling a scream. She had been willing to go to the wall for him. He meant everything to her, but apparently she meant nothing to him. She needed to do something. Anything. She paced the bedroom floor, back and forth. She ran downstairs to the kitchen, picked up a glass, about to throw it, changed her mind, then ran back up to her room, outraged.

How could he take the first drag, knowing what that stuff does to people? The answer was apparently Gregory thought nothing of his own life, much less that of his family, having made the decision to kill himself slowly with crack. Tuesday decided, if that was what he wanted to do with his life, so be it, she thought; but he is not going to wreck our lives in the meantime.

She also came to the conclusion that he should do it quickly, and that she would assist in the effort. Why put off the inevitable? she thought. Suddenly, all of the pent up rage bubbled up like a volcano inside of her about to explode. As it started to boil over, she could feel her face getting warmer. At that very moment, Tuesday resolved to help Gregory meet his maker.

First, she needed someone to stay at the house while she was gone. Picking up the phone, she dialed.

"Hey, Nancy, can you do me a favor?" Tuesday explained how she needed to run an errand, to which Nancy agreed.

"One of the boys has a school trip, and you forgot to pick something up for lunch again, right?" Nancy teased, coming through the front door.

"Something like that, yes," Tuesday answered, maintaining her composure. "The boys are asleep, and I should be back in an hour or less. Thanks, Nance. I owe you one," said Tuesday grabbing her keys, and running out the side door.

Driving to a certain section of town where it was purported that anyone could get drive-through service, as long as they had the means necessary to make a purchase, Tuesday sat unnoticed, and watched, studying the scene, learning how drug transactions were made. She had read in the newspapers about these street corners where crack and cocaine were sold out right in the open. Exact locations were also televised on the eleven o'clock news. After witnessing more than four drug-buys, she felt confident enough to make one herself. Tuesday started her Jeep, drove around the block and nervously pulled alongside of one of the five young men standing on the corner and handed him a twenty-dollar bill. He gave her two miniature plastic zip-lock bags containing a white powder, which she assumed to be crack or cocaine. Having accomplished that, she drove away and headed back to East Oak Lane, the adrenaline racing through her veins. However, before going home, she made a stop at the supermarket and bought milk, cereal, something for the boys' lunch, a box of mothballs and a box of rat poison.

Thanking Nancy for her help, Tuesday closed the door after her and calmly pulled her deadly components out, placing them on the coffee table. Emptying the contents of the tiny bags, she scraped a few crystalline mothballs until she had enough to fill one entire baggy, then she opened the rat poison. It looked more like oatmeal. Who would sniff this, she thought? Remembering the mortar and pestle she used to ground herbs and spices with, she ran to the kitchen to get it. Returning, she sat, grinding up the rat food into microscopic toxic bits. Then, mixing all three of the ingredients, she poured the entire venomous combination into the two little bags. Upstairs, she went to Gregory's closet, placing them in the inside jacket pocket of one of his favorite outfits.

The next day GB arrived on time, with his lawyer in tow. The smell of homemade, chicken noodle soup rushed out the door, as Tuesday opened it to let them in. Hoping Adam was nearby; she took a quick glimpse of the street, looking for his car. She'd called him at the last minute, for moral support.

Mr. Herman M. Meanly, Esquire; stepped across the threshold and stopped, blocking the entrance of GB who almost ran into him from behind. With outstretched arms, like a crossing guard, Meanly inspected the area; craning his neck to look right and left into the nearly empty rooms. Ready for anything, he checked behind the opened door as only a good scout would, seeking out any signs of ambush, making sure, as their leader, they weren't stepping into a trap. Moving cautiously further inside the house, Meanly finally gave the all-clear sign, signaling GB to come in.

Holding a dishtowel, she watched him closely. Tuesday hadn't liked him before they met. He'd pulled too many shenanigans; she thought, and was obviously hell-bent on making a bad situation worse. Now she despised him.

Although…the possibility that he may be off his rocker; did occur to her just then. She closed the door and turned to face them, standing with her arms folded.

"What is the meaning of all this? Why are you," she asked pointing at Meanly, "here in my house? And why didn't he take his clothes when he had the chance? Do you know about the damage he did here? Do you know that he took all of my belongings? Do you know that? He tried to destroy this house. And I don't know how all this is affecting the children."

Meanly stepped forward.

"Everything that you just said is your word against his. And to answer your other question, I'm here to protect GB from you."

She threw her hands in the air. "Protect him from me? I was the one who was beat up. I was the one whose ass was kicked every other day. And you're here to protect him?" She screamed like a mad woman.

Meanly's look confirmed her outburst. "As I said before, it's your word against his. By the way, where are the children?"

She hated this man. It was the first time in her life that she'd ever met a person and hated them within minutes. "It's none of your business. I don't hear their father asking about them." She felt outnumbered.

GB said nothing at all. Meanly motioned him, and he went upstairs to get his clothing and other things, making several trips back and forth.

In the interim, Meanly removed some official looking documents from his pocket, and served her with them, explaining that she would not receive any support except through legal channels.

She read the papers. Among GB's list of demands, the first was that he insisted she file for and pay for the divorce. Two, she should have custody of the children. In fact, she could have full custody, but he would not pay a dime towards any support of any kind at all, unless she filed. She sighed. He was really putting her in a financial squeeze.

Reading the petition, she wanted to know what she and the boys had done to deserve this?

She looked up to see Gregory and Meanly carrying out her bed, sheets flapping in the wind.

"Community property," Meanly called out when he saw her mouth open.

"He's entitled to half of everything."

She followed them to the door as they carried out the other parts of the bedroom set. At the door, she saw that Gregory had brought along a U-Haul trailer attached to his car. She watched as he carried out the teakwood coffee table and fireplace set. He then went into the backyard, removing the patio furniture, and placing it alongside the other items in the trailer.

Smiling, Meanly gave her a curt bow then opened his car door. "Goodbye for now." Then tipping a make-believe hat, added, "The next time we meet, hopefully, will be in court."

CHAPTER THIRTEEN

As the weeks progressed, slowly but surely, each fixture and every appliance was repaired in order of priority. One step at a time, Tuesday reminded herself, making sure to stick to her goal of rehabilitating the house, getting everything restored, in order to get by, to survive; leaving the spikes locked in the windows as security.

Today they were in her colleague's office for what was probably the last meeting pertaining to her divorce, which would be declared final in another week or so.

"The final divorce papers will be served on Greg in a few days," Zoë said. She seemed to be coming to the end of her diatribe, but one could never be sure. She evidently loved the sound of her own voice, and had a habit of going on and on. Pausing, she took a gift-wrapped package out of her drawer, and handed it to Tuesday. "You'll be a free woman by October 15th. Until then, here's something I thought might cheer you up on those down days."

"Thank you, Zoë for all you've done; you've been a cheerleader all along. I should be the one giving you a gift, not you to me. But, thank you anyway."

A voice came over the intercom. "You have a call, Ms. Wright, line five."

Zoë reached for the phone.

Tuesday took it as a cue, making a beeline out, zooming back into her own office. Of all nights, tonight she didn't want to work late or take it home; but as the dutiful junior partner she'd sat politely, listening as Zoë made another one of her long, boring speeches. Thank goodness the intercom had provided her an escape.

She sat at her desk, reflecting, on the pile of papers in front of her; many of them petitions for divorce.

Divorce. What an ugly word, she thought, but probably a good match for all the equally ugly events that surround the word. What does 'divorce' mean in Latin anyway? Good riddance? She lay Zoë's gift on her desk, picked up one of the pages in front of her and read it.

Atkinson vs. Atkinson; sounds more like a championship prizefight. At the final hearing sometimes a client beamed brightly as if they'd just triumphed over a great battle.

Ding!! And the winner and new champion is…

Judging from the smiles on some of their faces, a prizefight was exactly the way it was for a few of the men and women whose cases she'd handled.

Somehow, in her case, she personally didn't feel as though she'd won anything.

The experience was more like that of a funeral. The end of her marriage made her think of all the things people said or wrote about death, about certain phases in the mourning process everyone goes through and the adjustments made during each phase; the same mourning and the same adjustments she'd experienced, of late. In spite of the fact that there is no such thing as a divorce funeral, there are those friends and family members who will mourn with you, who will offer consolation, because they truly understand your loss. They know that divorce isn't a remedy or a cure for what ails you. Unlike getting rid of a cold, it is a major part of your life story, much like the death of a loved one. When it happens the survivors must go on. The death of her marriage was as real a loss to her as the loss of anyone she'd ever known. Indeed, it was worse, because a part of her had died along with her marriage. A part of her husband had died and a part of their children, too. Sadly, she'd witnessed the innocent light in her boys' eyes flicker and die out, to be fleetingly ignited during brief supervised visitations with their father.

She grieved for the dead and buried family, now gone forever. So much for divorce.

Replacing the Atkinson page in its spot, she remembered the present from Zoë, and opened it. There inside was a beautifully hand-inscribed poem, framed in wood with gold gild tracings, which she read aloud.

A Silver Tongue

An angel sits near
speaking soft words of wisdom into my ear.
Exposing what I know in my heart,
aware of what I fear to hear.

The angel knows no matter how hard I try,
I've yet to get over you.
For there is a part of me that lives,
that believes you still love me, too.

"Have no fear, my dear," the gentle angel says,
"Soon there will come a day
when that part will die and wither away;
and in its place, a feeling strong,
a new heart will be born,
a new love you will see.
And, no longer will your heart be torn.

Use these words of love anew,
these precious pearls,
to quench your thirst and heal your heart;
my dear, keep them close to you."

■ Author unknown

Too bad, she thought. The author deserves some acknowledgement. She admired the poem and its frame again.

Zoë was right, it was just the kind of inspiration she needed. Placing it next to the recently taken photo of herself and the boys, she studied the image of her new family, her face slowly forming a smile.

Tuesday picked up the phone and dialed. After a few rings, it was answered.

"Zoë. I was just calling to say thank you for the gift, the poem, it's lovely. And thank you again for helping me get through this. I consider you a friend."

"Why thank you, Tuesday."

"I mean it Zoë. I know for a fact that I could not have made it without you and the rest of my friends and my family. I feel like at last I've come to the end of this mourning period I've been in, and that I'm finally able to continue on with my own life, separate and apart from Gregory. And you helped me get there."

"Good.

"Thank goodness, Lady. At times, I wondered if you were going to make it. It was touch and go there for a while," Zoë, uncharacteristically, joked.

"I think we'll be okay."

Tuesday thought for a moment, then said, "I *know* we're gonna make it."

"Very good," Zoë laughed out loud, something she very rarely did. "Good for you."

"Listen," Tuesday said looking at the clock on her laptop computer, "it's about time for me to head out of here before the after-school teachers start charging me a dollar a minute late fee. For me that's four dollars a minute, Girl. Let me pack up to go. I'll talk to you later. Bye."

On the drive home, Tuesday thought about Greg. She'd been waiting for a telephone call ever since he left that day, more than a week ago, with that big-mouthed lawyer of his; imagining each day someone calling to report his death; perplexed to find his blood work indicating the ingestion of a lethal mixture of carbons and other chemicals one normally associates with rat poison, mothballs, and crack cocaine. The coroner would also find the same chemical reaction lining the inside of his lungs, thus, the assumption would be that he'd made a bad drug buy.

Instead, she hadn't heard anything, which meant he was still alive, maybe shopping for new clothes right now, probably having smoked the stuff and gotten a little sick, or maybe he hadn't gotten sick at all. Maybe he'd enjoyed smoking the poison; maybe what she added made no difference at all.

He had to have seen it by now, she thought.

At home later, Tuesday lay in her new bed relaxing, reading a magazine, the kids asleep, when the phone rang. She answered it to find Larry on the other end.

"Hey Sis, how you doin'? Spoke to GB the other day, he told me that he moved out his clothes and everything last week. I just wanted to check in with you and let you know that no matter what happens between you and GB, you will always be my sister as far as I'm concerned."

They chatted for a time with Tuesday answering his questions and living the fear once again; humiliated once again. When she told him about the double life his brother had been leading, Larry offered some advice.

Carefully, he explained, "You should know there is nothing you can do for him at this point. No one can change another person. If a person is going to change, he has to do it for himself. What you need to do is get help for yourself right now, Tuesday. Call Nar/Anon, they can give you some guidance and help."

"Nar/Anon, what is that?" Something about it was vaguely familiar, but she wasn't sure what.

"Nar/Anon is like Al/Anon, but for narcotics, where groups of people meet everyday, in different places, all over the country, to share their experiences as a husband, or wife, parent or child of an addict. They're able to talk openly with other people who have had the same kind of thing happen in their lives," Larry spelled it out for her, hoping he'd hit a chord with Tuesday.

"Do you really think a meeting is going to help, Larry? I don't know. Why would I want to go there? I'm not the one who needs help."

Just thinking about the kind of people who probably attend those meetings gave her a chill.

"Besides that," she told Larry, "it's never actually been confirmed by Greg himself that he even used the pipe. So, why should I subject myself to a meeting with husbands and wives of hard-core users? It's embarrassing."

Larry couldn't understand, she thought. She was a professional, and Lord knows who she might run into going in or coming out of one of those places.

"Larry, I appreciate your advice, but Greg is obviously not a hard-core user. It's not as if he's on the street, or stealing money and jewelry, and using it to buy drugs. You understand what I mean? Thank you anyway, but I don't think I need to go."

Larry was starting to get anxious, he didn't want to overstep his boundaries. Yet, he wanted to make his point and try to help his brother's wife.

"But, Tue, you just told me that GB stole your money, and your jewelry. So, we know he's bad off. Anyway, the real reason you should go is to get help for yourself, Tue. You need to understand the nature of what you've been dealing with. What do you know about drug addiction, huh? Probably, not much. At the meeting you'll meet people like you, who had *no idea* about what was going on, but once they did, they realized that they needed help dealing with it."

"Okay, okay, Larry, I see what you mean." What he said made sense. She had to admit to herself that she hadn't recognized the signs in Greg at all. And, that even if she had, she wouldn't have known what to do about it.

"I understand, Larry, but if I do decide to go to one of these meetings how in the world would I find out where they're held?" she laughed. "There's no listing in the telephone book or anything like that," she said cynically.

Larry laughed, too, happy to hear her laugh about something. He answered, "Actually, Tuesday, I looked it up while we were rapping, it's 1-800-662 HELP here. It's probably the same number for you. You have a pencil and paper to write that down?"

"Yes, I have it."

"All right, then, you make sure you call. I know you may think you don't need to, but you do. Call the number, please. I'll holler at you later. I love you, take care of yourself and the kids." Then he hung up.

Tuesday sat there looking at the piece of paper. "Hey, what do I have to lose," she said aloud to herself. Exhaling, she picked up the phone to dial.

CHAPTER FOURTEEN

Gasoline fumes emerged from the car, filling his nostrils, as GB loosened the gas cap. He chuckled, feeling good as he emptied a two-pound box of sugar into Tuesday's gas tank.

"I only wish I could be there to see her stupid, ugly face when the engine seizes up on her dumb ass. I can see it now, her driving along—in the car I paid for, the one I made the damn monthly payments on," he murmured.

Replacing the gas cap, he tightened it, wondering how many miles she would be able to drive before the sugar dissolved and the Jeep stopped running. Not that it matters to him really. After thinking about it, he should have added that crap she planted in his jacket pocket, whatever the hell that was.

He started to get angry remembering the package he'd found in his clothes, when the mental image of Tuesday came to him--her face flying forward, crashing through the windshield of her car. He smiled at the thought. The bitch wouldn't know what hit her. The fucking car would just stop; stop, just like that. The thought of it made him chuckle again; glad he'd thought to bring the sugar. So, if he didn't get her tonight, her own Jeep would get her tomorrow.

Soundlessly, he made his way over to the ashcan on the other side of the house, lifted the lid and disposed of the empty box, clapping his hands together; he brushed away the last few granules of sugar. The harder they fall, the sweeter the revenge, he laughed to himself. He knew what he had to do this time. And he had to do it now, before the divorce became final.

After pouring the sugar into her gas tank, his plan was to wait outside there in the dark, knowing that, in due time, she would come out to empty the trash, which would give him the opportunity to get inside. His plan was to go straight up stairs to the guest bedroom next to Daniel's and creep quietly into the closet. Once there, he'd crawl through the opening in between the walls, where she said the ex-slaves were supposedly hidden back in the eighteen hundreds, and hide there until they were all asleep, then he'd put his master game plan into action. Deciding to wait near the pool, he slipped into the yard, pulling a folding chair into a darkened corner, where he sat and waited. That was okay though, because he had time and now he was in a better mood. Not only was he happy about the sugar, he was also proud of the way he was patiently waiting for Tuesday to come out of the house. No theatrics, no need.

Looking up, he could see her through the kitchen window; doing the dishes he supposed. Watching her aroused an opposing combination of abhorrence and attraction. On the one hand, he always knew where she was coming from and having a relationship with a person like Tuesday was comforting, and dependable; on the other hand she made him sick, always nagging about the same damn things, like taking out the trash. That's how he knew, after being married to her for seven of the worst years of his life... he knew she would eventually come out to empty the trash. The evil, horse-face, onion-breath slut always made sure the trash baskets from every room were emptied every night; claiming the smell of what was discarded inside made her want to puke, then she always added, "It draws bugs, too," in that irritating voice of hers.

    "As far as I'm concerned, she's the trashy bitch drawing the bugs," said the little voice. GB concurred. Knowing exactly what he had to do; dressed in pressed khaki pants and a lightweight sweater, carrying a few necessary tools in a small chamois bag, he waited, ready.

    "GB Washington," he told himself, "you are seeing things clearly for the very first time."

    Her view obscured by the armload of trash she carried, Tuesday struggled to open the side door. Holding the bags and trying to turn the doorknob at the same time seemed impossible. Everything was harder to do now. Raising her knee to help balance the double load, she held the bags closer to her body with her one arm, giving her a free hand with which to undo the top latch. Then, bouncing on one foot, she finally turned the bottom knob. She was doing things she never had to do before; things like taking out the trash, pumping her own gas, taking the car to the shop and….

    Finally, getting the door open, Tuesday stepped out, lingering to take a deep breath. Thank goodness this year was almost over. Next year has to be better, she thought.

    Just then she felt the rush of chilly, early October air, as it entered her body through every opening in her skin, and went directly to her brain. She held her head back, away from the trash she carried, and took another deep breath. Snow, she thought, wondering if it's going to come early, like last year. Dressed only in a long tee shirt and shoes, she shivered as the cold, moist air engulfed her, encircling her, trying to push past her to make it's way into the house. Realizing that she was standing there with the door wide open, she pulled it shut behind her, just enough so that the lock wouldn't catch, then went down the few wooden steps to the side of the house.

The side of the house being dark, almost completely black, where the cans were hidden, made her a teeny bit nervous. When a flicker of light from the street lamp reflected off the shiny top of one of them, she used those few seconds to hurriedly place the bags of trash into one of the cans. That gave her just enough time.

Turning to go back into the house, she saw that the wind had blown the door open. Intuitively, a fear raced up her spine as she looked around for any signs of Gregory having been there.

"What!" she said aloud, turning in all directions. It's as if he's right here, she thought, swearing she'd gotten a whiff of his Old Spice cologne.

She stood, listening, only to hear the rustling of the leaves on the trees. A few cars whizzed by. Eventually, she was able to reconcile herself to the fact that since she hadn't really closed the door tightly, a small gust of wind basically pushed it open. Then, something flickered down from the sky, reminding her of snow again. Shoveling snow. Something else she never had to do before. Sighing, she resigned herself to the fact, and walked back around the house to go in, looking down the driveway, counting the fifty-feet to the street. This driveway was going to take a lot of shoveling, but it was either shovel it or pay someone else to do it. Neither was a satisfactory alternative.

Then she thought about Gregory, wondering what he was doing right now. Her eyes filled with tears when she thought about the person she'd married almost eight years ago. Seeing him at their final divorce hearing made those years seem like another lifetime ago, because the Gregory she knew was very different compared to the imposter she saw today.

Breathing in the cold night air, she became unsettled again, thinking she'd heard something.

"Oh no, stop it Tuesday. Stop it," she demanded of her self. "He's not here. You've got to stop thinking about him," turning, she went up the steps. "Don't waste your time thinking about him," she muttered. Why bother? He doesn't care about you or his own children."

Firm in that knowledge, she ran into the house and slammed the door shut. After locking it, Tuesday shook her head, laughing at her own wild imagination.

So strongly had his unique aroma been imbedded and ingrained into her memory banks, she thought she smelled him even now. It seemed almost as though he was standing next to her at this very moment.

She turned quickly to make sure he wasn't there.

"Now that would be scary," she breathed out, relaxing.

"Shit," he cursed, after bumping his head. Tuesday had come in right behind him, so he hadn't had time to get upstairs. Instead, he'd had to run and hide behind the basement door before she saw him. Quietly, he'd crept down the stairs.

"Shit," he cursed again, "stuck in the dark-fucking basement. Shit."

Standing slightly stooped because of the low ceiling, he'd heard Tuesday come rushing back inside, slamming the door shut. He wondered what had frightened her to make her run inside like that. A sound caught his attention, causing him to look up, watching the floor overhead. It's her, he thought.

As if he could see right through the old wooden beams, Greg pictured everything she was doing above him. Amazingly the floor seemed to reverberate with each one of her evil footsteps, he believed. Allowing the sound of her sinister trail to lead him into the family room, he imagined her standing in front of the fireplace; striking one of the foot-long fireplace matches, then lighting one of those store bought logs with it. Eventually the real logs would catch and the entire room would be aglow from the flame. That had been *his* custom for so many years. Feeling the anger start to emanate from the back of his neck, his jaw began to tighten. It was *his* family room and *his* fireplace. Again, he looked at the floor above when he heard her start to move. But she didn't go far. He pictured her putting the matches away, then standing in front of the fire, warming her hands. Her hands were always cold—the sign of a witch.

"That's what she is, a goddamn fucking witch," he mumbled to himself. "First, the witch put me out of my own house, then tried to kill me with some fake-ass poison cocaine shit. I don't know what made her think she was ever goin' to get away with that shit. How could she think she could put me out of my own house... then try to do me in, and think she could get away with it? The goddamn stupid ass witch had better hope for a quick spell or be able to pull some heavy duty shit out of a hat, cause she's goin' to pay for all of this shit dearly."

He promised himself then, that he was going to get her for what she had done to him if it was the last thing he ever did. The bitch will never know what hit her. He smiled at the thought of what he had in store for her.

"Apparently," he spoke with his finger pointing to the low ceiling, "I didn't do enough to bring you to your fucking knees the last time," he started to pace back and forth.

"You would think that between sawing the fucking desk and all your dumb-ass case files and fancy goddamn law books, would have been enough, but noooo… *you want more.*"

The bitch deserved everything I did, he told himself. I only did it because of everything she'd done to me. She put me out of my house.

He stopped pacing and stared at the ceiling. It was supposed to have been unbearable for the little princess bitch to deal with, she was supposed to have finally conceded and moved out of the house, back to West Philly where she fuckin' belongs. He didn't understand what had happened: She'd stayed in the house anyway, after everything he'd done. Obviously, what he'd done wasn't enough. Now he planned to really make it unfucking-comfortable. Startled, he was brought back to the present when he heard the heels of her shoes clicking against the hardwood floor. She was on the move again. Anxious to leave the basement, he again began to walk back and forth in small circles.

"When is she going to go up the fucking stairs?" he demanded, whispering.

"What is she doing, anyway? The whore."

Just then the furnace came on. He watched the caged heat leap around inside the mammoth, foreboding metal thing, with its many alloyed arms protruding in all directions, then amused himself by tracing the path of one of the tentacles. He could smell the grimy dust as it started to burn inside the furnace's oven. This must be the first time she's used the heater this season, he thought. That's good. It means her money is tight.

In the darkness, he bumped into a water pipe sticking out, up from the concrete floor, stubbing his foot.

"Fuck," he ranted in a low murmur, sucking in large amounts of air and blowing it out between curses, bouncing up and down on one leg. He blamed her. Bending over, he massaged his banged toes through his sneaker. To balance himself, he held onto the pipe just above his head. The pain in his foot caused him to become even more upset and angry, turning it into a passion, which made his blood boil. The heat rising to the top of his head made it ache. He started to sweat, blaming her. He stopped kneading his foot and stood straight up, hitting his head on one of the wheels sticking out from the furnace valve.

"See what you can do with this, bitch. You're so fucking smart."

He turned the wheel in the opposite direction. Then, he walked over to the other side of the furnace and turned the spindle of the valve on that side, too. An unexpected thought occurred, he stopped to think. He had to remember everything he'd done just in case it was up to him to undo it. The point was to get her out so he could move in. He looked up. It was simple. All he had to do was wet his finger with a little saliva and make a big letter X in the dust next to each of the rotated valves. Doing it, he felt better.

His attention turned as he heard the evil footsteps walking off to the far right of him. He looked up, angry, again. Why wasn't that whore upstairs with the children, anyway? Wasn't it bath time? What was she doing, leaving them alone all this time? The witch.

Finally. He heard her as she made her way up the stairs, seeing her with that prissy way she had of holding the stairway railing with one hand while the other hand dangled from her wrist as if it were broken, swishing her little butt from side to side, as if she owned the whole fucking world. He started to become sexually aroused.

Distracted when he heard the water start to run through the pipes, his body relaxed. As the watery sounds traveled through the pipes, he could tell then she was getting their bath ready. Eventually, he heard the gleeful sounds of his sons at the approach of their mother. He knew the time was almost right for him to leave the dank, dark, gloomy room and go quietly up the stairs as planned. He waited until he heard the faint sounds of his children splashing in the bathtub. Knowing that the bathroom door would be shut to retain the warm moist steam, he also knew Tuesday would not leave the children alone as long as they were in the tub. Now is the time, he thought.

Quietly, he crept up the back stairway and made his way into the closet and through the small opening in the far wall.

CHAPTER FIFTEEN

Earlier, Tuesday shivered, not sure if it was from the cold air or the fear she felt. Leaning against the door for a moment, then, regaining control, she decided it was the cold air, and to reassure her nerves, as well as to get warm, she went into the family room where she lit a log in the fireplace. Before long, a calming glow emanated from the opening in the wall and created shadows that bounced and changed rhythmically. There was something about the smell of the burning logs and the crackling noises of the fire that soothed her soul. This feels good, she thought, rubbing her cold hands together warming them over the blaze; after their bath we'll all come down here to read in front of this cozy fire.

She would put on her pajamas too, and they would have a pajama party. They would lie on the pillows lined up in a circle on the carpet (her new do-it-yourself sofa) where they would read.

Satisfied by her decision, she smiled, warming her hands and watching the flame, looking into it dreamily; grateful to be thinking about nothing in particular, except what book she would read to her children later. Hearing the boys playing, she looked up, reminded that it was time to head upstairs.

The soles of her heels clicked against the hardwood floor as she walked to the bottom of the stairs. Just then she felt a draft.

"I'd better turn on the furnace, too." Tuesday turned the thermostat dial then headed up the staircase to the second floor to bathe the boys and get them ready for a good night's sleep.

They loved bath time.

"You all are Mommy's little water babies," she cooed as they splashed in the bubble bath and played with their toys. She scooped up a handful of water, letting a few drops land on Gabriel's head and waited for a reaction. Tuesday watched the drops of water run down the little one's face. He looked over his shoulder and then above his head. The expression on his smooth face seeming to say, "Where did that come from? And what was that anyway?"

Tuesday laughed. The others looked then as Tuesday cupped both hands with water and said that she was going to drip some on each of their heads. They let loose with peals of laughter.

She began to sing. "This is the way we wash our hands, wash our hands, wash our hands." The children joined in, but Tuesday was distracted by the sound of something in the background.

"What is that? Thunder?" she asked, knowing the boys were clueless.

The rumbling continued, and, as she listened, seemed to get louder.

"What is that?" she asked, cocking her head to one side, leaning toward the closed bathroom door.

The children looked confused.

"Thunder, Mommy," answered David.

Tuesday shook her head.

"I don't know, I'm not so sure it is thunder, Baby. Mommy had better go check it out."

She stood. The sound was very close by; she was sure of it. She helped the boys out of the tub and they began to towel off.

As the last of the water gurgled down the drain, she opened the bathroom door, steam escaped from the room. "You guys put on your pajamas. I'll be right back."

It was then that she realized the loud rumbling noise was coming from inside the house, not outside, as she had assumed.

Alarmed, she ran quickly down the stairs to investigate. Going from room to room, she realized it was most likely coming from the bottom floor.

Holding an ear to the basement door, she stood motionless, listening, without a clue. It suddenly occurred to her; Gregory could be down there.

"He's been on my mind all night," she mumbled. Then she heard it again. There it is. What is that noise?

Kneading the front of her tee shirt in-between cold, damp fingers; with her free hand, she gently cracked the door open, then, stopped. Pressing a hand to her chest, she tried to stop her heart from tearing through her skin. She exhaled, not realizing that she'd been holding her breath the whole time, knowing she needed to go down there and see what was going on.

"Who's there?" She called, buying more time, still.

"Greg?" She whispered.

He can't be down there. No way, she thought, checking behind her.

Opening the door wider, she turned on the light.

Leaning forward, she peered down the stairs, hoping to see or hear something, without having to actually go down into the basement.

Suddenly, there was a loud *boo-boom* sound like crackling thunder and lightening, causing her to jump.

At least now she knew it wasn't Greg. Laughing, she calmed down somewhat. But, then what *is* going on down there? Who... what is making that racket? *Thor?* What's Thor doing in my basement?

Placing one foot in front of the other, she tiptoed down the stairs, moving slowly and cautiously, as if the slightest noise might cause the thunder-god to get even more upset. Stepping carefully, descending one by one, as quietly as a ballerina, she thought of having smelled Greg's cologne... and stopped.

No, it couldn't be him. He wasn't allowed within a hundred feet of the house because of the restraining order.

She sniffed the air. It was thick and gritty in her nostrils, a dry dusty scent. The surrounding air was warming. The rumbling *boo-boom* thundercloud-noise was getting closer as she descended the stairs.

A bomb.

She froze.

Would Gregory go that far? A gush of cool air on her back made her turn to gaze up toward the open doorway and think longingly about the telephone sitting on the kitchen counter just at the top of the stairs, the line just having been reconnected. Maybe she should call somebody. But who? Adam? What did he know about houses with loud noises in the basement? And, besides that, how long would it take him to get here? Maybe Derrick could take a look. He's right across the street. Something in her said no, you'd better check this out right now.

Convinced, she muttered, "You're halfway there now, you might as well take care of this yourself, right now." Gathering her resolve she continued down.

Besides, she reasoned, what could Derrick do about this? It sounds like an earthquake and feels like one, too. Gripping the banister with a death-choke, holding on for dear life, she could feel the tremors traveling through the wood, tingling her fingertips. She wanted to turn and run back up the stairs, but knowing she couldn't, continued down, step by step.

Whatever it was—whatever it was that was happening, she wished it would stop and just *go away*. A few steps away from the bottom she stopped to look around.

Something is weird, she thought.

Loudness boomed all around her, pounding, pulsating, growing, pushing its way through the gritty heat-saturated air; all bass, no treble, a deep thrumming, thundering reverberation. The experience was very similar to the way she felt walking through the colossal heart exhibit in the museum, where a speaker set inside the massive right ventricle sent the same pulsing, vibrating sound throughout her entire body.

What is going on? What's making all this noise?

Standing at the bottom of the staircase, she paused to scrutinize the rest of the room, afraid.

The throng of the giant heartbeat seemed to be coming from every direction of every corner in the basement; from where it emanated she couldn't tell.

Searching for a sign, surrounded by cold granite fortified stone, the kind of dungeon-like place where a person may have been tortured, shackled to the walls, she drew in a breath of bravery. There were only two possible causes for all of this commotion, as far as she could surmise; the pipes or the furnace.

A quick examination of the pipe overhead revealed nothing, no leak, nor steam escaping from anywhere.

Moving toward the furnace, she could see a raging fire inside. Bending to get a closer look at the fire, she tried to figure out how the furnace could be the cause of what felt like an earthquake in her house. A fire is supposed to burn in the furnace, right? she asked herself. But this fire seemed rather large. But, was it larger than usual? she questioned herself. She didn't know.

Straightening, she put her hands on her hips, sighing. Everything else about the furnace appeared to be okay as far as she was concerned.

"What am I supposed to do now?" she asked the furnace.

Just then, it moved, looking as though it shimmied.

"Whoa!"

Her eyes widened, she stumbled backward, away from it.

"Let me cut this thing off," she mumbled, turning toward the stairs, heading for the thermostat.

Bounding up, two at a time, she used the banister like a pole vault to give her extra momentum and lift. Halfway up she tried for three.

The toes of her foot, not quite making it, did not touch the edge of the step solidly enough to give her the leverage she needed to bring her other foot forward. Instead, her foot landed solidly one step below. Unfortunately, the forward momentum caused her shin to hit the protruding edge of the step at breakneck speed.

Screaming as a thousand nerve endings sent pain signals leaping from the spot on her leg directly to her brain, bringing tears to her eyes, she froze.

An earsplitting fracture of a thundercloud cracked in the background.

Afraid to move, weak from the pain, beads of sweat broke out on her forehead. The pain in her leg had brought thoughts of anything else to a blinding halt.

She stood with all of her weight on one leg, holding the other in midair, knee bent, writhing with throbbing tenderness, clinging to the banister.

As the noise from the basement continued to get louder, slowly the pain began to subside.

Remembering, after a moment, there was a red emergency shut off switch near the top of the stairs; she limped upward.

Using the banister as a crutch, Tuesday hopped up one step and then another, finally reaching the top, and at long last flipped the switch. It made an audible, *click,* but nothing else changed.

The noise, seeming to have followed her from the basement, she looked down at it as the clamoring continued. Turning back to the switch she flipped it again. Then again. *Click. Click. Click.*

It was as if the switch was not connected to the furnace at all. The entire house began to shudder.

"Don't panic," she said aloud.

Tuesday wiped the dust from the label on the red box surrounding the switch and read it. It had yellowed and was worn thin from age, but it listed the phone number to the heating maintenance company. She repeated it a few times, trying to memorize it, heading lamely to the phone on the kitchen counter. Tuesday dialed; praying for a connection, praying for someone to answer, praying the company was still in business.

Tapping her fingers and leaning against the counter as she waited, trying to maintain her cool, she was frantic, nonetheless.

The microwave clock read 8:35 p.m. She wondered if anyone was there at this time of night, or if they worked around the clock, or what if she gets an answering machine, then what?

The tremors had gotten worse, too. She could hardly hear the ringing on the other end of the line because of the noise.

The boys had felt them, too. In their five and six-year-old minds, where gentle-voiced lion-kings, fairies, flying horses and flesh-eating hobgoblins were real, the house had obviously come alive. Trembling and crying, the youngsters ran to her, wrapping their arms as tightly as they could around their mother's legs. She grasped the phone tightly, while squelching a pain-filled scream.

After what seemed an eternity, someone answered on the opposite line.

"Hello, you've reached Acme…" The HVAC technician began.

"Help!!" Tuesday shrieked.

Startled, the 23-year-old displaced cowpoke sprung forward from his chair, as the blood-curdling scream caused him to take the phone away from his ear. He jumped to attention.

It was times like this he wondered why he stayed. For the second time that evening he asked himself, why was he still here? Why, (in the City of Brotherly Love) when he really craved the prairie? He dressed the part: Worn out blue jeans and a wool flannel shirt, cattle-roping duds. He'd been relaxing, watching the Dallas Cowboys and resting his $485 leather boots on the desk. Sighing deeply, he pulled the phone back near his ear.

"Can you hear it? Something's happening here, and I don't know... I don't know what." Tuesday was frenzied by everything happening at once; the cacophony of her children's cries, unsure of whether or not her leg was broken, the thrumming, pounding sound coming from the furnace was almost too much.

"What?" he answered, "Lady, your scream knocked me outta my chair. Now what can I do for you?"

Just then the Cowboys made a charge, taking them all the way from midfield to the end zone. Wide-eyed, he forgot the voice on the phone; mesmerized by the action, his hand moved toward the telephone cradle to hang up. As the play ended, he remembered. Returning to a sitting position, he placed the phone to his ear again.

"What is she goin' on about?" he grumbled, "This woman is completely incomprehensible." Leaning forward to concentrate, he tried to hear, but the screaming in the background made it almost impossible.

"I... "The..." She screamed even louder.

"Anoiseiscomingfromthefurnaceandthewholehouse isshakinglikeanearthquake!"

He held the phone far out, and away from his ear, looking at it until she stopped. Using the space between his shoulder and his head as a place to rest the phone, he nonchalantly cradled it. Then, slowly picking up a toothpick, he carefully cleaned under his fingernails. He wasn't havin' it. Whatever her problem was, he wasn't about to let it interfere with his mood, or his football game. No. He stuck the toothpick under another one of his nails and scraped. Trying to keep the irritation out of his words, he politely informed the voice on the phone, "Miss, I don't understand. Could you say that again?"

"Listen!"

Leaning back in his chair, trying to stay calm, he rubbed his brow, and let out another exasperated sigh.

"Listen, Miss, all this hollerin' is gittin' us nowhere. Now, could you please just calm down and try to tell me what's goin' on? Now just calm down."

Then he added, "Please."

Tuesday, on the other end of the phone, was ready to go berserk. Standing in her kitchen, she was desperately trying to make this man understand the nature of her emergency. Taking his advice, she spoke calmly.

"I'm going to hold the phone toward my basement door where there's a loud racket coming from the furnace. I want you to hear it and tell me what to do. Okay?"

"Okay, Miss, that's better. Go ahead and let me hear it."

She did as she was told.

The smell of hot metal scorched the insides of her nostrils, leaving a gritty, burnt taste in her mouth. The four boys stood in tiny puddles of water that had dripped from their wet bodies, shivering as they huddled around her knees, even though the house had been getting warmer and warmer by the moment.

He held the receiver closer to his ear and turned down the volume on the television set, hearing the noise clearly.

It was finally starting to make sense... becoming dangerously clear.

"Okay. Okay. Right. No it can't be," he muttered mostly to himself. "Hello. Miss?"

She put the phone back to her ear. "Can you hear it? That's my furnace." She held the phone out again. Did he understand now? If not, why not? He had to have heard it. Was he stupid? She started to hang up, frustrated by dealing with this man who refused to comprehend.

He stood. If only the woman on the other end would just give him a chance to think. "I heard it. Give me your name and address, in case we lose our connection."

She rattled it off quickly.

Blinking rapidly, his eyes darted around the office as he thought. Things were starting to click. Okay, so the furnace was making a noise. All right, he thought. Was that really the furnace he had heard? That couldn't be right, but that's what she'd said.

'Anoisewascomingfromthefurnaceandthewholehou sewasshakinglikeanearthquake'.

A noise. Okay, yeah, the furnace. But makin' the whole house shake?

She listened as the voice commanded. "You have a red emergency shut-off switch for your furnace, probably near the cellar door. Hit it now!"

"I did that already," now she was really starting to panic. "Nothing happened. I think the switch is broken," she said. A feeling of helplessness washed over her.

"What else can I do?" she asked limply.

Now it was his turn to shout.

"Take the phone with you to the furnace. There are about seven valves on the pipes extruding from the furnace and one of them is a manual shut-off, which you need to close. I'm gonna walk you through it to make sure you turn the right one. Turning the wrong one will only make the situation worse."

"I can't take the phone, it won't reach, besides, I think my leg is broken. I can't make it down there and up the steps again and the noise is getting louder. The house is shaking even more now. What else can I do?" she pleaded, starting to break down.

Oh hell, he thought. If that was the furnace making that sound he'd just heard, she'd better run for cover. Suddenly, he was moving back and forth as he spoke, thinking of her best options.

"Listen to me carefully," the voice on the other end soothed calmly, gently now.

"Something's happened to your furnace, a vacuum maybe. Whatever it is, I can hear it getting worse. We can't waste any time. This is a bad situation, Miss.

"Now I want you to listen to me."

He inhaled. "Who's there with you?"

"My four children and myself. We're the only ones here."

"Can you get everyone out of the house?"

She answered that she could.

"Okay. Then you get everyone out of the house *RIGHT AWAY*. I think your house is about to blow. Do you understand? Drop the phone. Get out of the house. Now!"

She didn't waste time placing the phone back on its cradle. The last thing she heard was him asking if she understood, as she released the phone from her grip and peeled the panic-stricken boys from her legs. She told them to run out the door, and away from the house as far as they could. She pushed, and all five headed for the door.

Oh God, Tuesday thought, her mind racing, please, help us--this, her mantra, as she hobbled toward the door. "Please help us, God. Don't let us die."

Bits and pieces of her life seemed to fly before her eyes as she moved. They're wrong, she thought, going as fast as she could toward the door. Your entire life doesn't go flying by, only slices, here and there. Even then, they are in no particular order, just a random sequence of events, like a slide show where the transparencies are in complete disarray. Why does this particular situation fly into view and not another? She wondered. Who knows? Her mind raced about—thoughts and pictures incongruous to her present state of affairs. The only connection between each snapshot was that each had something to do with getting her to this point--smack in the middle of a life-threatening experience.

     The man on the telephone hoped they would make it out in time. He listened, even after he'd heard the thump of her phone against the floor. As loud screams came through the receiver, he remained. Standing with the phone to his ear, he took no notice of the television and the twenty-five yard Hail Mary pass that had the football crowd up on its feet. He waited, missing it when the kicker sealed the fate of the game by adding another two points to the score. Then he'd heard more screams, and running feet. He waited, as the running screams became fainter. As expected, he heard the piercing sound of a smoke alarm, then another.

     Holding the phone away from his ear, he endured, until he couldn't make out anything apart from the earsplitting sound of the alarms.

     Then he heard a *click*…

     Dead silence.

CHAPTER SIXTEEN

GB had been using his hands as a pillow, lying on his side on the floor in the once flourishing Underground Railroad station hidden in-between the walls of his house. The coolness of the floorboards felt good against his body. There was a gentle breeze too, moving between the planks of rough-hewn wood tickling the hairs of his nose with a one hundred and fifty-year old scent of musty pine. His eyes were open, but couldn't see much of anything beyond his hand. And he wouldn't have been able to see that much if it wasn't for a yellowish sliver of light that peeped in from the cracks surrounding the Alice-in-Wonderland-sized entrance.

The dark, tight enclosure had a calming effect on him. He was getting sleepy. A low thundering sound roared in the distance, catching his attention. Moving his hands, he put his ear to the floor, trying to listen, becoming perfectly quiet, eyes closed, he held his breath in an attempt to hear better, trying to figure out from where that low, monotonous, rolling sound was coming. Then, he thought he felt something brush by him, as if another person were sitting next to him. Spooky, he thought, wiping his arm. Although the room was too dark to make out anything, of course he knew he was alone. After a while, he heard Tuesday and both sets of twins in the bathroom and concentrated on trying to make out the muffled sounds seeping in through the cracks.

Peals of laughter filled the air and floated down the hall toward him. He heard water running and smelled the tangy sting of a sudsy bubble bath. They were all just old enough to think they could wash themselves.

Sometimes, when he'd bathed them, they would snatch the soapy wash cloth right out of his hand and scrub their own faces. He smiled at the thought of it. No matter how often it happened, it was always a delightful surprise when they showed that kind of independence. His boys. Those were the happy days, before now. The joyous bibble-babble of the children continued.

There was that thundering sound again. He was curious to know if they'd heard it. He knew Duce and Daniel would be afraid, they always ran and hid whenever there was thunder and lightening, but no one seemed to notice at all.

He spent the next few minutes speculating about the distance of the thunderstorm; not recalling hearing or reading anything about it on the weather channel. But, you never knew about the weather these days, just one more thing you couldn't count on. He waited, listening.

Something was crawling up his leg. He shook his pant leg. Then pulling and tugging, he struggled to get at the hem of his pants, barely able to bend in the tight space. He felt it crawling higher up his leg, toward his thigh. He shook his pants again. Slapping his knee, GB felt it spatter. An ambitious spider, he guessed, shaking out the remains.

He was starting to unwind again. Now, he wondered how the abolitionists could have fit more than one person in here. Taking it easy, he sat contemplating the average height and size of the previous slave inhabitants of this small space. Somewhere, he'd read that at times an entire runaway family would take shelter in one of these teeny places. He didn't see how, there was barely enough room for him in these so-called 'guest' quarters. What a misnomer.

    The walls were too close together for one thing; he knew, because after he'd squeezed through the tiny portal opening, he'd gotten stuck. Then he'd had to compress his shoulders to mimic an old, hunched-over woman so his shoulders would be small enough to allow him the ability to turn. Like a cursing and angry Charlie Chaplin, stupidly bouncing from wall-to-wall, he'd twisted and turned his entire torso and then did a kind of flip in order to face the door so that he could get out when the time was right, surprised that Tuesday didn't hear and come to catch him in there. During all of that, to make matters worse, he'd accidentally hit the damn door, causing it to slam shut; then, after all of the clamor, the automatic locking mechanism went into gear; which meant he was in there for the duration.

    "Relax," his mind said, *"no biggy. No sense in making a commotion trying to get out now; you can relax for now; cause that shit-for-brains-whore is going to get hers. Don't worry, sleep on the floor and wait for them to leave in the morning. Work your magic in the house then, and when the bitch leaves for work in the morning, the car will do the trick. Break out after that, and do what you came to do. Get her out of this house once and for all, the witch-bitch."*

    Smiling, he thought about all the things he was going to do before he drifted off to sleep.

    It wasn't long before he dreamily became aware again. How much time had passed? An hour? More? He wasn't sure, but now he was awake, his eyes adjusting to the darkness. The little strand of light peeping in from the crack seemed to have gotten brighter.

Just then, he felt a trembling motion in the floor; starting to get up, he bumped his head on a ceiling rafter. At the same time he heard singing, coming from the bathroom. That means I couldn't have been asleep too long, if they were still in the bathroom, he thought, although... sometimes the boys insisted on playing in the tub until their skin turned into prunes, so it was no telling. The area beneath him trembled again. He put his ear to the floor. Didn't Tuesday hear it? Obviously not, she and the boys seemed to be oblivious to the noise as far as he could tell. It wasn't so low and monotonous anymore, either. What could it be? It was starting to get louder.

His patience was starting to wear thin. He felt like going to see what was happening, but changed his mind. Let the stupid whore handle it, he thought. That's right! She's so damn smart. Let her handle it. She's the smart-ass lawyer.

Eventually, the low thundering sound was replaced with a loud racket. It could be coming from inside the house, even, he was thinking. Couldn't the dumb bitch hear that? What was she, deaf or something?

He waited, finally, hearing her go downstairs, the horse-faced slut. A short time afterwards, he'd heard the boys run down, too.

Twisting and turning, he sat up; knees locked together with just enough room to allow him to lean against a wall with his knees pushed tightly to his chest, his feet pressed against the opposite wall. The trembling had been replaced with an earthquake. The cool breeze he'd felt earlier had been replaced by warm air.

She should have taken care of this, whatever it was, by now. He was beginning to have his doubts about Tuesday and her ability to control the situation. He sat there waiting, nonetheless.

After a while, it became too much. The thundering sound was deafening, seeming to echo off the walls of the cramped space. He felt trapped, wiping a bead of sweat from his brow. The house was getting too warm. Noises, including those of his children came from someplace below him. What could be going on? The whole house was starting to shake.

GB sniffed. Was that smoke? He sniffed again. Is the house on fire?

What if the house had caught fire? Then he'd better get the hell out now, he thought, moving to get up. Regrettably, GB turned in the wrong direction; now he was stuck again, facing the back wall.

"Open this damn door!" he demanded, unable to budge his wide shoulders wedged in-between the narrow space. To get situated so that his feet would face the door, he finally succeeded in doing the opposite of what he'd done when he entered the hiding place, with a sort of flipping motion, he gingerly kicked at the door a few times, trying not to damage it. Remembering the possibility that this could be an emergency situation, he let his foot slam into the door so hard, it flew off its hinges and bounced off the wall, way across the other side of the room.

Shouting for help as he twisted and turned, GB was able to quickly maneuver his way back out, feet first. Straining with both arms above his head he pushed his hands against the wall and slithered out on his belly, eventually getting to the point where he was finally able to stand upright.

Stretching felt good. Now he could go see what the hell she'd been doing all this time, "The stupid bitch," he murmured, heading for the stairs.

There they are. He stared down at Tuesday and the boys scurrying toward the front door.

Out of the din of confusion Tuesday thought she'd heard another, different, sound. Something... seemed to be out of place, causing her to turn and look up at the top of the stairs. Seeing Gregory there baffled her at first, then suddenly everything made sense, that somehow he'd been the cause of all this. Distracted, Tuesday skidded on a wet spot and fell grimacing, her eyes squeezed shut.

"Go!" She waved from the floor. "Keep going. Run to Aunt Nancy's house.

Look at her dumb lazy ass fall, he smiled; better yet, she should have hit her head and died. Serves her right, he thought; I wish I'd taken a hint from O.J. and gotten rid of the greedy, low-class, slimy hoe a long time ago. He grinned as the picture of his hands closing in around her throat crystallized in his mind.

Still looking up, Tuesday fixed her eyes on him, dragging herself to her feet. Oh my God, Gregory, she was thinking, as they watched each other for a long moment.

"Gregory?"

His features were changed, so much so, she hardly recognized her husband. In a moment of realization, it occurred to her that he wasn't Gregory at all, that GB had completed the transformation, devouring any and all remnants of Greg's soul.

He screamed at her from above. "I found that package you left in my clothes, you silly bitch. What'd you think? You think I was just going to snort the shit and die, dumb ass?" GB swaggered down the stairs after her, taking his time.

Feeling a murderous hate emanating from him she backed away slowly.

"Where you think you going, Tuesday? You can't run. I can see that," he smirked. "I'm going to kill your ass tonight, with my bare hands." He continued down.

She heard what he said, but her mind raced back to what the man said on the phone, that this place was about to blow up. The loud blaring screech of an alarm went off just then, and she turned to hobble out of the house as fast as she could.

GB, deciding to increase the speed of his stride, was halfway down when he felt a hand on his shoulder shove him hard.

"What the.." Turning to see who it was, he slipped on the wetness, bouncing down the balance of the stairs, breaking a rib in the process. One by one, other alarms resounded, like so many toy fire engines doing wheelies throughout the house. Groaning, concentrating on the location of the pain, he leaned against the bottom step for support. Legs outstretched, he worked to catch his breath.

The earsplitting screech of a smoke alarm directly above his head startled him. The slight movement sent twinges of agony shooting through his skull like a razor-sharp knife. A thin haze of smoke caught in GB's throat, choking him.

Moments later, the tumultuous sound of the monster heartbeat brought him back to his senses. What was going on? he wondered, grabbing at the pain in his side, afraid to breathe, afraid to move.

Listening, he heard a thunderous sound, like a flight of F-16 fighter-bombers, it seemed to him; where the low approach of their sonic boom seemed to roar closer and closer causing the house to make a long, low rumble and shake that seemed to last a lifetime. Then suddenly in his mind, the F-16's let it rip, dropping their entire payload on him there in his home. At that very moment a blast came--as the furnace, beneath him, exploded.

Jeffrey, who was pulling the evening shift at the Acme Heating and Maintenance Company, hung up and called the fire department as soon as the phone had gone dead. He knew there would be a tremendous fire, especially if it was one of those big old homes; that is, if his guess was right, that her address was in East Oak Lane. In speaking with the fire department dispatcher he'd explained the situation and warned about the possibility of a second blast coming from the gas main. He also told them that he was pretty certain that everyone, the woman and her four children, had gotten out of the house in time; or so he hoped anyway. After that, he'd hung up the phone and jumped into his pickup to drive out and see what he could do to help.

Outside of her home, running, hobbling, down the sidewalk, Tuesday called for help fearing that GB was coming after her. In protecting the children from the explosion, she chased after them, trying to shield them with her body, to prevent them from getting hit with the shards of glass and pieces of wood that were being fired at them like shrapnel, when she tripped and fell, hitting her head on the pavement. The pain... the white-hot pain of a lightening-bolt zigzagged from above and penetrated her skull. She moaned. Looking up from the ground, Tuesday saw the look of terror on the faces of her children. Then, reaching up to hold them, it felt as if her arms weren't long enough, as if she were floating away. She looked at them again, but they seemed to be moving farther and farther away from her. Slowly, she lost consciousness then blacked out.

Nancy put her book down on the table next to her, and looked out her window to see what was going on.

The neighbors, after hearing what sounded like the blast of a building implosion, looked out their windows and came to their doors to see four pajama-clad boys they recognized as the Washingtons run screaming into the street.

"Derrick!" Nancy called, "Derrick!"

She ran and opened her front door where she saw the children running, frenzied, squealing and crying in the direction of her house. They ran up the few steps and straight into her arms.

"Derrick!" Nancy hollered again, louder this time. "Oh Jesus," she looked around, "Tuesday." Holding the shivering boys, she asked, "Where's your mother?"

"She fell on the ground over there," one of the frightened boys answered.

Derrick looked up from his basement workshop when he heard his name being called; then brought his hammer down hard, driving the nail into the wood, but also banging his thumb in the process. His balled fist came directly to his mouth, where he withheld a shout. Immediately dropping the hammer, he sprang from the spot where he'd been building a shelf.

"What? What is it?" he asked sucking his thumb, rushing through the kitchen, after he'd heard the worry in Nancy's voice. When he got there, he saw her kneeling at the open door.

"Jesus, you scared me! What are you yelling about? Did you hear that noise?" Confused, he asked looking around, "What are the boys doing here? Where's Tuesday?"

"I don't know. I heard someone screaming, the boys say she fell, maybe that was her, go check," she said pointing. "I'll take them inside."

"Okay," said Derrick. "Call the police, too."

Before Nancy could get the kids inside and shut the door there came the loud blast of a second eruption.

Derrick turned to come back inside. Nancy handed the phone to him. Dialing it, he said, "Gotta call the fire department first, then go over there." No sooner had he'd hung up when they heard the sounds of fire trucks arriving.

"We're gonna need some help with this one," the fire chief said after analyzing the situation. "I can see that right now."

Looking around from the burning house to his men running line, he could see this was going to be a long night. He radioed the dispatcher to request additional support, estimating the need for another five engines, at least.

"Okay, thanks, over and out," he said, and securely fastened the Velcro microphone holder back to his jacket, returning his attention to the house.

"Chief, there's a man and some other people over here who say the woman we found unconscious is the owner of the house. Looks like she got a pretty good bump on the head from a fall. They say she lives here with her four kids. The kids are okay."

"Good. That's good to hear. What about anyone else; do we know if there was anyone else in the house when this started?"

"No, Chief. The neighbors say she lived there, just her and the kids. She and her husband were divorced or just about, anyway. The kids say no one else was there."

"Okay, so there's no need to send any men in. Good job. Thanks. Now, let's put this fire out."

The chief stood thinking as the firefighter returned to his duties. He was depending on the children who stated that there was no one else in the house, but they were just kids so he couldn't be positive. He hoped the neighbors were right about the number of people in the house, because the woman they'd found was down for the count. He thought back to the dispatcher, who'd said there was a caller who'd spoken directly to the woman. She'd reportedly said it was just her and the kids. That's enough, the fire chief decided, seeing as how the neighbors had confirmed the caller and the kids, he certainly wasn't going to send any of his men into the blaze needlessly.

Thank God, he thought, when he heard the sounds, the answer to his call for backup, in the far off distance, getting closer and closer. They're on their way.

She'd heard the sirens of several fire engines roar by, as she leaned back relaxed, in the bed reading. They seem pretty close actually, she thought dismissively.

Bruce, her husband, was piloting a scheduled overnight flight. The girls were supposedly asleep in the adjacent bedrooms. Jackie Blacksmith, about to snack on a bag of bar-be-que flavored potato chips, had the rest of the evening to herself. Who knew better than she, being a doctor, how adversely those chips affected her arteries, her cholesterol count, and the size of her waistline, but it was one of her secret passions. And, whenever Bruce was gone overnight, the chips bought her solace. Tearing open the fresh bag released a salty mixture of potatoes and hot sauce into the air. Crunching down on her first delicious bite, and returning her attention to the study of a newly-modified surgical procedure she would be performing in the morning, she smiled sardonically to herself.

The television was also on, for company. There was breaking news, interrupting the show. She looked up when she heard the reporter mention something about East Oak Lane. Saving her page, she placed the surgical manual face down and used the remote control to turn up the sound, in order to hear what was going on.

Staring back at her from the TV was an animated reporter, seemingly distressed, commentating in front of a fiery scene, which showed a house up in flames. In the background, Jackie saw emergency crews and cameras, and firemen with hoses running every which way. The surrounding area looked remarkably like the block Tuesday lived on. Jackie decided to call and check on her, but did not get an answer. After several more unsuccessful tries, she decided to call Jerry Cunningham. He was Greg's friend. Getting no answer there either, she decided to call Tuesday's friend Millie, to see if she knew anything, or had been watching the news.

Millie picked up the portable phone, which was ringing on the nightstand next to her bed. "Hello," she said into it.

"Millie? This is Jackie Blacksmith. We met this summer at Tuesday Washington's party. Remember? This is going to sound strange, but do you have the TV on?"

"No, it's not on. Why?" Millie took the phone away from her ear and looked at it. Putting it back, she asked, "Who is this again?"

Hurriedly Jackie said, "I know this might be wacky, but, it's me, Jackie Blacksmith. Turn on the TV to Channel Two, and tell me if that isn't Tuesday and Gregory's house," she ordered.

Still holding the phone to her ear, Millie went downstairs into the den, where she switched on the television set, turning to Channel Two. She stood staring at the scene.

Jackie wondered if she had been disconnected. "Millie? Are you still there?"

"Yes," Millie answered, "I'm here. I'm trying to look, to see if that's the house or not. What makes you think it's Tuesday's house?" she asked.

"Because. The reporter said it was East Oak Lane, and I'm sure you know the problems they've been having. I wouldn't be surprised at anything Greg did these days. I'm her physician and you're her best friend. You know what he did a few months ago. He's capable of anything. It wouldn't surprise me to find out that he set the house on fire. Besides that, look when they pan the area. Doesn't it look like... Wait... Listen..."

Millie turned up the volume.

"Girl, did you hear that?" Jackie asked her. "They said they think it may have been set deliberately. I told you. Greg set that house on fire, Girl. He's been acting real crazy lately," Jackie said in a tone, which underlined her authority on the matter.

"Let me call you back." Millie pushed the button to disconnect the line, then dialed Tuesday's number. When she didn't get an answer, she sat down on the bed and said a prayer for her friend.

Inside the house, the fire raged unchecked in the basement after the first explosion. Something... he was now sure, some *thing*, had given him a hard push and at this very moment it hovered over him, eerily blocking his exit. The little voice silenced. GB watched as the hazy figure divided, becoming two, then three, then more than he could count, surrounding him within a flash.

A second detonation came just then; the force of it causing pieces of the ceiling to give way, to come crashing down on GB, who fell to the floor on his knees looking up as the obscure figures seemingly conducted, calling the fire to life, orchestrating his funeral.

Coughing and shaken, GB watched as gaseous flames leaped up through the unsealed spaces separating the floor from the edges of the settled wall. As graceful as tiny little ballerinas, the miniature flames danced individually and then held hands, totally encasing him in a fiery ring of sapphire and rubies and tiger-eyes. The cloudy figures continued to conduct in a giant, swirling, hideous mass. And, so directed, the fire rose, and the room became a burning, powerful, inferno all around him. He felt suffocated, as if he were being swallowed whole.

Thick smoke invaded his lungs, suffocating him even more. Rubbing his burning eyes and gasping for air, vomiting when the rank fumes created a toxic mixture of burning paint and varnished lumber, GB stood, having used everything he could to get himself into a standing position as the area beneath him became burning hot.

All of a sudden, the thunder quieted.

The lights went out, creating a black hole there in the room sucking up all sound. Even the battery-operated smoke detectors silenced, one by one. The shaking stopped, too. The only sound, the peaceful crackling hush of fire.

Cool air swept in. Through the whirpool of smoke he could see the same open door his family had exited through to safety only moments before. His only escape, he thought, taking a step towards it.

Coughing again, and spitting large pieces of the gross acrid tasting mortar, which had fallen into his mouth, he knew he had to get out before there was another blast. Aided by the staircase railing, he pulled himself up with one hand, afraid to move the other, which was shielding his ribcage. The excruciating suffering in his side was worse than GB had ever imagined; a searing pain that stabbed at his insides.

Suddenly, the thought hit him like a hard knock upside the head when he remembered the basement.

He'd turned a valve leading to the furnace because she was getting on his last nerve. Now, he wondered whether turning those other spindles had been a catalyst having anything to do with what was happening now, here in the house. Had he caused this fire?

Using what little oxygen remained in the room, he went back down on his knees, crawling over ceiling rubble toward the door. Calling out a whispered plea, "Tuesday," as the hazy, churning mass of inhumanity settled down over him.

"Help me, please." He was almost at the door, when a heavy sustaining rafter beam, as old as the house, broke away from the wall, falling onto the rubble just beyond.

Another, smaller sound escaped his lips this time.

"Tuesday," he whipsered, swallowing instinctively as more splinters of wood and plaster fell and dropped into his mouth. Unable to breathe, vomiting again, slowly he became aware that now, his fate was sealed, and headed toward him. The doorway was blocked. The rumbling sound getting nearer and nearer. Paralyzed, he watched as one of the hazy figures seemed to energize the beam, helping it, guiding it toward him.

He watched, unable to move a muscle as the massive girder toppled forward in a straight path en route for him. It rolled hugely, intently, forward.

"Forgive..." was all he had time to murmur before it broke his neck and decapitated him in the process.

Soon, the whole room became one vast crematory, burning him entirely, leaving nothing behind with the exception of a few charred, sizzling bones and ashes and a set of teeth, including one gold canine.

THE END

Addendum

I hope you enjoyed reading this book. During my research, I came across a widely publicized court case in which the details of a disorder known as Battered Woman Syndrome were first nationally proclaimed. Of late, statistics have borne out the fact that middle-class and upper-class women, including professionals, are battered at almost the same 35% rate as their lower-class counterparts. To help answer the question, which pops up in most minds as to why these women stay in abusive relationships, social scientists have developed a behavior model of battered women. This model may also help explain why abused women often return home. It is my sincere hope that this book also helps to explain why women stay in these relationships.

According to Dr. Denyse Hicks, founder of the <u>African American Women's Mental Health Authority</u>, *A Silver Tongue*, has given a voice to the over 50 million Americans experiencing the affects of trauma and substance abuse in any given year. Only one-fourth of them actually gets help. Part of the reason is the stigma attached to the imperfect image of needing help. Men and women of all races would benefit from the wisdom shared in this novel. She goes on to say how each reader can gain the valuable lessons of seeking professional help, breaking the cycle of silence and secrets, and identifying signs of destructive behaviors.

To the many faceless women and men suffering from domestic abuse, remember: *"That which does not kill us makes us stronger."* -- Nietzche

Use this convenient coupon to order books by Marlene Taylor. Send check or money order

TO: ℗shun Dynasty Publications   Visit: www.asilvertongue.com

P O Box 2574
Bala Cynwyd PA 19004 to order your copy.

Please send me the books I have checked below.

☐ **A SILVER TONGUE** a daring new psychological suspense. In a world where a little voice seems to be running the show, this is love at it's most obsessive; a twisted, gritty tale of sex and violence, full of suspense, set in a quiet Philadelphia neighborhood. Bizarre is the only way to describe the perfectly executed turn of events in this compelling narrative. $9.99 U.S. / $1199 CAN ISBN 0-9677679-1-1

☐ **LIFE IS WHAT YOU MAKE IT, DARLIN'** Bruce is every woman's dream of a husband, except for one thing; a secret he has held for all the years of his marriage. Love unexpectedly reaches new heights as together Bruce and Jackie struggle to work their way through the heartache and terror of the haunting past that jeopardizes their world. $9.99 U.S. / $11.99 CAN ISBN 0-9677679-0-3

I am enclosing $ _____ (Please add 2.00 to cover postage and handling. No cash or C.O.D.'s).
Prices are subject to change without notice.

Include recipient's address:
Name _____

Address _____

City _____ State _____ Zip _____